The
FAR
EUPHRATES

The

FAR
EUPHRATES

Aryeh

Lev

Stollman

RIVERHEAD BOOKS

a member of Penguin Putnam Inc.

NEW YORK

1997

Riverhead Books
a member of
Penguin Putnam Inc.
200 Madison Avenue
New York, NY 10016

Copyright © 1997 by Aryeh Lev Stollman

Library of Congress Cataloging-in-
Publication Data

Stollman, Aryeh Lev.
The far Euphrates / Aryeh Lev Stollman.
p.   cm.
ISBN 1-57322-075-2 (acid-free)
I. Title.
PS3569.T6228F37   1997   97-167 CIP
813'.54—dc21

Printed in the United States of America
1   3   5   7   9   10   8   6   4   2

This book is printed on acid-free paper. ∞

Book design by Judith Stagnitto Abbate
Map by Jackie Aher

For
Deborah and Samuel Stollman,
and for
Tobias Picker

Contents

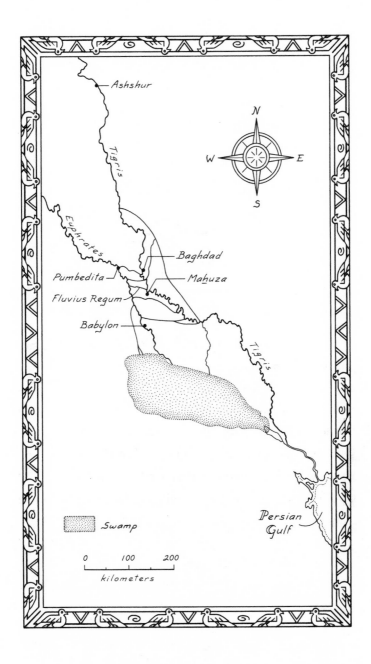

Author's Note

This novel is a work of fiction. The events described are imaginary, and the characters are fictitious and not intended to represent specific living persons. When persons are referred to by their true names, they are portrayed in entirely fictitious circumstances; the reader should not infer that these events ever actually happened. The events portrayed herein with regard to the terrifying fate of the twins and the Gypsies who arrived at Auschwitz are based on historical fact.

Menashe Lorinczi:

We heard a terrible cry. The Gypsies knew they were going to be put to death, and they cried all night.

They had been at Auschwitz a long time. They had seen the Jews arriving at the ramps, had watched the selections where the old people and the children went to the gas chambers. [And so] they cried.

And when the Gypsies cried, all the twins heard them.

And even though I was a child, only nine or ten years old, I understood.

from *Children of the Flames: Dr. Josef Mengele and the Untold Story of the Twins of Auschwitz,*
Lucette Matalon Lagnado and Sheila Cohn Dekel

Through wisdom a home is built, and by understanding it is established, and by knowledge are the rooms filled with all precious and pleasant riches.

Proverbs 24:3–4

The

FAR
EUPHRATES

Windsor

A

t dessert following a holiday lunch, I over-heard my mother mention yet again her concern about me.

The Cantor had baked petits fours iced with musical notations. My mother picked a phrase off the serving platter and gazed at it. I remember her taking a small bite into the treble clef and saying uneasily to Hannalore, the Cantor's sister, something about my being *un rêveur.*

My mother's French was limited, but she knew a few words which she sometimes scattered in her speech. Though I had my suspicions, I immediately asked what *un rêveur* meant.

Hannalore answered, "Nothing, *mein Liebchen*. Dream on, dream on." She passed me the dessert platter. "Now, please, eat some music, *Alexandre*."

Although nothing further was said at the time, I think that shortly thereafter Hannalore proposed her plan and my mother agreed to take me on a little pilgrimage.

The summer before I started grade school, my mother worried obsessively about me. I do not know precisely when this worry began, or when I myself realized it was there. I did not know what it was all about. On physical grounds I could not have given her much reason for concern. Except for a series of minor ear infections, I was a healthy child, and from all indications I was an attractive little boy. I was not effeminate; I did not lisp or play with dolls. I was not cruel to smaller children or animals, although, it is true, I had no brothers, sisters, or pets to be cruel to, and I was, it is also true, something of a loner. For the most part, I did not show great interest in playing with other children, though as later events would show, I was capable of strong friendship.

Overall I was a well-behaved and intelligent child. I had quickly and even hungrily mastered two different alphabets while still in kindergarten, and this, as I remember it, brought me much praise from both my parents. My mother baked me sugar cookies in the shapes of those transmuting and buoyant letters that drifted down to us from the seafaring Phoenicians, and my father had started reading Genesis with me, slowly, in its original tongue, where the dotted vowels clustered like bees around the honeyed consonants. We read each sentence together, carefully, first in Hebrew, then in English, and finally in German.

My father was determined that I learn as many languages as possible. Moses had spoken all seventy known in his time, and my father had resolved that I start out in life with at least three. He believed, as a matter of course, in the ascendancy of the earliest of tongues, the Semitic *Ursprache*, and the dominion of all speech in every imaginable form, even after the sin and dispersion of Babel.

He told me, to my great amazement, leaning across the dining room table, how God's sweet letters were also the powerful tools whereby He created light and everything in the universe: establishing the earth, suspending the sun and moon in the firmament for signs and for seasons, for days and for years. I would imagine these primordial letters, the symbols that brought forth not only the universe but, to my even greater astonishment, my very own existence, announced in the heavens—Aryeh Alexander ben Shelomo!—phosphorescent figures forming in the deep dark closet of space, an endless nothingness that as a child I could not conceive of any better than I can now. I had an inkling of it, though, at times when I was all alone, playing silently by myself, happily contemplating my luminous and celestial name.

I do not want to characterize my mother's worry about me as an irrational phobia, a strange fixation on her part, for we can never look back through so many years, or even directly at the present, and see ourselves from those infinite and always impossible vantage points that fan out from the very surface of our physical being—the everywhere and everything and everyone that is not us. Our souls—and I believe we have them in some fashion or other—together with those most personal and valuable of treasures, our accumulated knowledge and memory, are locked away, held prisoner within the disintegrating vault that is our corporeal selves.

At some point, the cause unknown to me then, my mother's worry began to consume her. Perhaps she began having sleepless nights, for I noticed she looked tired and worn. I would often catch her brown eyes watching me silently, or hear her say to my father or to friends, "He is too much of a dreamer" or "Well, he's in his own little world." These phrases, in retrospect, were a code for something she dared not speak, some looming tragedy for us both. I often heard the gentle bass of my father, or the reassuring lightness of women's voices, "Oh, well, Sarah, he's only a child. Children do that."

We lived in Windsor, a small Ontario city where my father was the rabbi. My mother's closest friend was Berenice, the Cantor's wife. They had developed a genuine friendship, of intense affection and respect, but also of compassion and mutual survival. Though both were Canadian born, these two women felt themselves outsiders, having grown up in the big cities, that is to say, in my mother's case (as in my father's), Toronto, and in Berenice's, Montreal. Together they believed they were in some kind of banishment from a better world. They referred to Windsor, on the toetip of our province, as "the Babylonian Exile" or "the Great Expulsion" or, simply, "another cow town." Sometimes they would relent in their criticism of that innocent and placid place, with its quiet streets and polite citizenry, and laughingly agree that Windsor was, after all, "not such a bad bargain," for it had been a generous and kindhearted matchmaker. It had brought my mother and Berenice together.

At that time my mother was in her late twenties and Berenice in her early thirties. My mother and Berenice had in common dark, gleaming hair. From time to time they would come home together from the beauty parlor on Friday afternoons, the Sabbath eve, with the same new hairstyle, giggling like schoolgirls. My father and the Cantor often called them the "Bobbsey Twins." But they were obviously not twins, and their differences were striking. My mother was of medium height and weight, and delicate in feature. As a rule she dressed modestly, in quiet colors. Berenice was a looming, hearty woman, almost a head taller than my mother. She always wore brightly colored dresses and had a weakness for expensive shoes.

"Let the truth now be known! Shout it from the rooftops!" she would declare, modeling for us her latest pair, often smuggled across the border from Detroit. "Berenice Seidengarn, née Rothman, *loves* shoes!" She would turn her long, narrow foot this way and that, as in the advertisements of those times, highlighting a sleek satin vamp or perhaps a towering heel. I suppose, though it never occurred to me then, that they must at times have made an odd, even a comical pair, these so physically dissimilar women parading through our town wearing their identical hairdos. Nevertheless, they still went about their daily lives in unison rhythms: they shopped together, took care of their households, worked for the community sisterhood. They gossiped between themselves when there was gossip to be had, something they felt they should not do with the other women in town. I saw how they were always polite and cordial to all. They believed in certain formalities and never called the older women in the congregation by their first names. They took their positions, as complements and extensions of their husbands' leadership, very seriously.

My mother taught at the synagogue's afternoon kinder-

garten, and her teacher's diploma hung in my parents' bedroom, in a gilt-edged frame next to their wedding picture.
On those occasions when my mother was unwell, Berenice
would substitute for her, a glorified form of baby-sitting,
since Berenice's knowledge of Hebrew was halting and rudi-
mentary. She knew, however, several songs with which she
could entertain the children, one of which was about a
whirling dervish of a train that traveled on its spinning
wheels the length and breadth of the Holy Land. She would
conga and boogie the perimeter of the classroom with all
the laughing kindergartners in tow, from the mountainous
glory of Jerusalem to the foothills of Lebanon. Her very
own brother, Berenice always told them, had moved from
Montreal and built a house near the Sea of Galilee.

Aside from their contrasting physical types, there was
another major difference between my mother and Berenice.
After ten years of marriage, Berenice had no children. For
this reason, I believe, she doted on me. "How's my boy?" she
would always say, or "How's tricks?" And if I had a small
cold or was the slightest bit sick, she would buy me a present. I looked forward to these easy ailments and undeserved
gifts. My mother would say gently, "Berenice, you are spoil-
ing him." But I think my mother was secretly glad that I
had this extra affection, this added attention, for in her own
obsessive worry she became almost afraid of me—to touch
me too much, or to caress me, though of course, like any
mother, she had done so from time to time, but less and

less frequently, as I remember it. Maybe, she felt, Berenice might help me somehow. And maybe, when Berenice hugged me—and she did so at every opportunity: "Come here, Alexander, give me a squeeze," enveloping me in her soft, heavy arms, in the floral scent of her bosom—it was proof I really was a normal child, a child others envied, that others would pray to God to have for their own. But aside from all her kindness to me and its implication, Berenice provided my mother with an unheeded warning against ingratitude, a form of greed and rebellion against one's Maker, and the taking for granted of life's blessings as they are mysteriously allotted and bestowed by divine plan.

My parents had wanted to have more children but were unable to after I was born. Years later, when I was a teenager and becoming a young man, what in the latter part of our century is still oddly considered the twilight of childhood, my mother said tearfully, in an uncharacteristic revelation that reached me as through a heavy curtain: "Berenice never had any children but always has a smile on her face. She never complains. Even now, with the Cantor so sick. She always tells me to count my blessings. . . . I try most of the time, I do, really, though perhaps not enough. Perhaps I've never been grateful enough—"

"And I am your punishment."

I amazed myself by interrupting her, by even speaking. I had at the time begun to isolate myself and severely curtailed my speech. Language had started to take up too much energy, exhausting me. I surprised myself even more by this harsh accusation hurled at my mother. But I truly believe, looking back, that I spoke this truth without malice or anger. It is too distressing for me to think I might have acted otherwise, with deliberate cruelty. For my state of mind then was not of malice or of anger, as it might have seemed at a first and casual glance. It was a process of withdrawal and internal realignment, a painful but necessary rearrangement of the hierarchy that exists in every breathing soul, the structure that mirrors the mystical shape of the living God Himself.

Even so, my mother was deeply wounded. Her tears abruptly ceased. She spoke distinctly, without hesitation, "No, Alexander. No. That's not what I meant." Her visits to my room, her attempts to engage me in casual conversation—a difficult, almost unnatural effort for my mother—stopped.

*H*annalore, the Cantor's twin sister, lived across the river from Windsor in Grosse Pointe, a wealthy suburb of Detroit that extends along Lake St. Clair. Hannalore was yet a different woman from either my mother or Berenice. My mother and Berenice, despite their own contrasting physical appearances and personalities, had, in my childhood perception, normal and similar accents, which meant feminine, English-speaking Canadian accents. They were, as far as I was concerned—though it was hardly true—of one language and one speech. Hannalore on the other hand spoke English with a foreign intonation and construction. She was a heavy smoker and had a husky voice. Like the Cantor, Hannalore spoke a perfect French and German, floating carelessly, spontaneously, from one language to the other. When my father would begin speaking the formal German he had learned from his parents and always sought to teach me, he would breathe deeply and pause, as if readying himself to move a heavy switch.

Hannalore was unlike Berenice and my mother in yet other ways. Like her brother, she was tall, thin, and white-haired. She worked as the head housekeeper for Henry Ford II. She always wore a stiffly starched white blouse with a high collar and long sleeves. Hannalore kept her religious background secret. Mr. Ford, she insisted, would not have tolerated her presence on his property if he knew (though she had no proof of this and it could, I've been told, be soundly disputed). To complete her disguise she wore a fine gold chain with a delicate cross around her neck, even on her days off, even when she visited her brother in Windsor. She seemed to revel in her little disguise, her long-standing ruse. That she could walk the luxurious streets of Grosse Pointe as a gentile appeared to give her great satisfaction. She once explained to my mother and Berenice, "When I walk down a street it is only me, old Mademoiselle Hannalore, *comprends?* And I am practically, deliciously invisible. A happy and contented ghost."

My father never openly criticized her little golden crucifix, though he was always staring, clearly discomfited by what he saw. Hannalore would return his stare from beneath her white-blond eyelashes, finger her little ornament, and then burst out laughing. Her large crooked teeth would reveal themselves, the same teeth the Cantor had. "Oh, *Rabbi! C'est juste un jouet—ein Spielzeug sozusagen!* It means nothing, absolutely nothing, to me! It is just two silly toy sticks hitting each other over their heads. Click! Clack!"

Hannalore lived on the Ford estate, in a wing of the main house, and worked there for many years, surviving Mr. Ford's first marriage. I had seen Hannalore on those occasions when she came over to Windsor on Rosh Hashanah or other holidays to have lunch with the Cantor and Berenice. Hannalore would arrive in a shiny sky-blue convertible that made me think she was rich, though before my little pilgrimage, this was still a somewhat abstract idea to me. Despite its being a holy day, she would park directly in front of the Cantor's house, next door to ours, precisely as we all returned from services. Neither my parents nor the Cantor and Berenice drove on the Sabbath or holidays.

Hannalore never came to any services, even to hear her brother sing, though it was well known that he had a beautiful tenor voice.

Sometimes even strangers would come to our synagogue to listen to him. One gentile woman, who owned an exclusive jewelry store in Walkerville, came once a year, on Rosh Hashanah, and brought her little daughter with her. From a distance—for they always sat in the back of the women's section and left before services were over—this strange-looking girl, dressed sumptuously as an infanta, filled me with a mixture of pity and horror. Sometimes I caught her staring at me.

My mother once asked Hannalore, "Why don't you ever come hear your brother? He is so wonderful! Everyone comes just to marvel at him." She then added in a stage whisper, smiling, "And you can skip my husband's sermon about God and His commandments and the Divine Presence in our world."

"Oh, I am not at all musical," Hannalore said. "Stone ears I have." She thumped the sides of her head lightly with her fists. "I used to think we were so much alike, but Bernhard inherited all the talent in the family! It is, of course, so unfair to be the twin without *anything* at all and with such a *terrible* voice as mine!"

Grosse Pointe

Other wealthy people like the Fords lived in Grosse Pointe: the Dodge family, presidents of other motor companies, insurance giants, a former governor, the movers and shakers of Michigan industry. One such industrialist who lived near the Fords' estate had an elderly maiden aunt, a woman "from the highest Michigan society—*sehr hoch-wohlgeboren,*" Hannalore said, who was believed to have special powers and, according to Hannalore, a little Gypsy blood. "It is this *soupçon* of ancient blood that gives her such powers. I know: I have had occasion to study these people up close. We lived right next to them in the camp. They do not trouble themselves so much about the past because, of course, what can you do about it? But they know the future. They see. They see!"

Hannalore claimed this woman was a true prophetess. And so, a few days after the holiday conversation with my mother, and the reference to my being *un rêveur*, Hannalore had driven to Windsor to pick us up and bring us to Grosse Pointe to see the great lady.

"*C'est vrai*, Berenice. *C'est vrai*, Madame Rabbi. I tell you this woman has said such things about my very self, no one else could have known them." For a brief moment while she was speaking, driving down our street, Hannalore let go of the steering wheel of her blue convertible, embraced herself with her thin arms, and shuddered. She shook her head as if to rid it of an unwanted thought. The car glided smoothly along the avenue. She took hold of the wheel again and whispered, "That woman can tell you *everything*." For a while Hannalore fell silent. She then looked in the rearview mirror and said cheerily to my mother: "She is a very strange creature—how do you say?—*une naine*, but inside it is all very kind. She is better for you and your son, Madame Rabbi, than a trip to Lourdes. Then, Madame Rabbi, you will know the future, which will open up like a happy flower, and you will not have to worry anymore."

Berenice, who was sitting up front with her sister-in-law, laughed. "I wish we *were* going to Lourdes. I haven't been to France in years! Perhaps we can go shopping before we come back home, to help remind me."

"I don't think that's so funny, Berenice," my mother said. "This is serious. You know how . . . how *concerned* I've been."

"I'm sorry, Sarah."

Hannalore turned around and looked directly at me in the backseat, "It will be *so* fun, *Alexandre*. You will not forget her."

Hannalore drove us over the Detroit River on the Ambassador Bridge. There were two ways to reach Detroit— one underwater via the tunnel, the route that was closer to our house and that my parents had always used, and the other by the bridge. But Hannalore was afraid of tunnels and any enclosed spaces. She would not even ride in an elevator. *"Jamais!"* I heard her emphasizing to my mother and Berenice. *"Niemals!"* She lowered her voice. "You know we were taken away in those terrible, crowded trains. That's where our father died. *Wie eine arme Fliege*—just like a poor fly."

My mother and Berenice both nodded solemnly, looking momentarily down in their laps.

That bright autumn day, my mother and Berenice wore matching sunglasses that Berenice had bought, brilliantly framed with rhinestones. The glasses sat like tropical butterflies, wings outstretched, on their noses. This was a typical extravagance urged on my more reserved mother by Berenice.

"I can't wear these, Berenice," my mother had said. "They're crazy!"

"Oh, they're just jewel tones, Sarah. They're pretty and fun. You can take them off when we get there."

My mother sighed and obeyed her friend. "You're such a bad influence, Berenice. If anyone were to see us!" While we were moving along in the car, my mother looked quickly from side to side, hoping no one would notice her as they drove by.

In my mother's lenses I saw reflected the broad greenish arc of river below us. During the ride over the Ambassador Bridge, my mother began constantly fidgeting, brushing back her beautiful dark hair and then turning to do the same to my hair. I tried to snuggle against her. "Now, sit up, Alexander. It's too warm. You'll get us both wrinkled." She straightened out my little false bow tie and the jacket of my white summer suit.

"Daddy doesn't need to know about this trip, sweetheart," my mother said as we drove above the choppy waters.

Hannalore laughed her hoarse polyglot laugh. "C'est notre petit secret!"

Berenice added, "Absolutely! The Rabbi wouldn't approve of Gypsy fortune-tellers!"

Hannalore turned abruptly and glared at Berenice. The car almost collided with the center railing. Hannalore slammed on the brakes and we came to a sudden stop. She turned off the engine. Cars behind us started honking.

Hannalore lowered her already low voice. "She is *not* a fortune-teller, Berenice. You must never speak ill of the Gypsies."

"I'm sorry," Berenice said. "I'm sorry. Really, I didn't mean it."

"Well, then. We shall let your indiscretion pass."

Hannalore restarted the car and drove on. The women were now quiet.

As we moved across the highest point of the arching span in the open convertible, I closed my eyes tight and imagined myself a seagull, gliding on air, letting the river breeze lift my wings ever higher. I inhaled deeply. I loved the sharp, damp smell. Then I transformed myself and became invisible—"without a physical body, but yet everywhere"—as my father had explained, like the *Ruach Elohim*, the Spirit of God at Creation.

From a great and wondrous height, alone, isolated from the earthly world, I peered down at an open basket of sky-blue papyrus holding three tiny women and drifting in the breadth of the Nile.

"Alexander. Alexander!" my mother's voice called up to me as they floated away to the land of the Gypsies.

I had never encountered such a heavenly vision as the innumerable castles and châteaus that we saw along the broad, leafy boulevard of Lake Shore Drive. Before we reached the prophetess's mansion, we passed the Ford estate. Hannalore, a cigarette in her outstretched hand, had pointed to a magnificent palace. "Look, *Alexandre!* That's where I live." On the other side of the boulevard was the beach and the tranquil waters of Lake St. Clair.

My parents, and the Cantor and Berenice, rented cottages on Lake St. Clair every year, but it was a different lake here in Grosse Pointe. Our own modest cabins were light-years away, on the opposite, Canadian shore, near the humble fishing town of Belle River.

Finally we stopped at a great iron gate. We were waved through and then drove along an oak-lined gravel driveway. At the porte cochere we were greeted by a uniformed maid, a woman almost identical in appearance to Hannalore, tall, skinny, and light-haired. She wore a starched white blouse with long sleeves, just as Hannalore always wore on her visits to Windsor. Hannalore and the maid greeted each other quickly in German. Another servant, a handsome young man in a tight uniform, came and took the car away. He winked at me as he drove off. We entered a grand foyer. Dark tapestries hung on all sides, between soaring stained-glass windows, the latter reminding me at first of those in my father's synagogue. But I quickly realized they were different. In my father's synagogue the windows portrayed scenes from the Bible: Adam, Eve, and the cunning Serpent with his mosaic of colored scales and tricks; Joshua blowing his glittery trumpet as the walls of Jericho tumbled down;

the angels floating up and down Jacob's Ladder, their feet never touching the rungs as they traveled between Heaven and Earth along the concourse of dreams. Here in Grosse Pointe, the windows showed nature in her variety: the moon on a snowy night, the sun over a green meadow, a nightingale in a flowering tree.

We were led up a wide staircase and around a hallway balcony that looked down over the grand entranceway. From that vantage point I saw the marble-tiled floor, where a great winged horse flew through a starry sky.

The maid led us down a dark corridor and knocked on a carved mahogany door. I heard no distinct answer, only a muffled sound. The maid opened the door. At the far end of an enormous and darkened room was a huge canopied bed, overflowing with red silk embroidered in gold. The heavy fabric was gathered above and around the bed. It reminded me of a great circus tent with an open front, its excess material flowing for some distance on the wooden floor like an outgoing wave. I did not notice anyone on the bed itself. It was covered in the same heavily embroidered cloth, and at first I thought there was no one to be seen.

My mother and Berenice were as overcome with all the dim splendor as I. They stood in the doorway and did not dare enter the room until Hannalore and the maid led them forward. The room itself seemed larger than our own house, and as my eyes adjusted to the dull light I began noticing other beautiful objects: a golden harp like a sail, delicately carved chairs and tables, plush velvet sofas, and a dark-blue chaise longue. All the window curtains were drawn, and the frail light in the room came from a large crystal chandelier that hung overhead in the great expanse before the bed.

Back on the magnificent bed I finally made out the tiniest of creatures, the smallest adult person I had ever seen. For a brief moment I was terrified, but then this person reminded me of one of those funny monkeys one saw advertised in the back of comic books, small enough to be held in a teacup or in a pocket, though in reality she was not quite that small. I succeeded in not giggling by squeezing my fists. She was, I realized, an old woman propped up against a satin pillow. She was dressed in the same splendid material as covered her bed. Her hair was wrapped in a shimmering gold turban. She coughed. It was a faint, hollow, monkey-in-a-teacup cough. Nearby, on the bed, was a large silver ashtray filled with butts.

"Is this the boy?"

My mother and Berenice were afraid to move or speak, but Hannalore led me by the hand to the bedside. "Yes, Mademoiselle Dee Dee. This is Alexander."

The seeress said, "Come closer. Climb on the bed so I can get a better look at you." She patted the space next to her. "Ah, a fine little prince! Are you scared of me? I won't bite you."

I thought of all the fearless boys in the Grimms' fairy tales my father read to me. He read these stories in the same earnest way he read me the Bible but with the languages in reverse. He first said each sentence in the original German, and then he translated it into English. Finally he translated it again, into Hebrew.

Ich fürchte mich nicht, I thought to myself, then repeated it out loud in English.

"I'm not afraid."

I climbed on the bed to prove it.

"Well, good." She stretched out her withered arm and touched my hands, while I sat kneeling on the bedspread. I was surprised that her hand was so warm.

Without any further introductions, she turned to my mother. "So? What's the problem? Out with it!" She cocked her head and stared directly in my mother's eyes, waiting, but my mother did not speak.

"You, young lady, are a bundle of nerves. Want a drink?"

"Oh, no. No, thank you."

"A cigarette?"

"Oh, no."

"Well?"

Finally my mother stuttered: "He's . . . a d-d-day-dreamer."

"Oh, God! Oh, God, don't be silly! All children are day-dreamers! All adults are daydreamers! When are we *not* dreaming? I don't have *time* for nonsense."

My mother looked cautiously at me and then back at the woman.

The woman shook a tiny gnarled finger at my mother. "Don't mince words. He can listen too. It's about him. There are no secrets here." Then she spoke very slowly, looking from my mother to Berenice and back to my mother again. "All secrets contain the seeds of death."

My mother glanced at Berenice for reassurance, but Berenice stood there like a statue. She had forgotten to take off her rhinestone sunglasses and looked silly and terrified at once.

My mother said, "I'm af-afraid for him. Afraid he . . . he might turn out wr-wrong. He doesn't always act like a regular child. There are things about him—"

The old prophetess rolled her eyes in despair. "You are such a stupid woman. Just stupid. Now leave the child with Mademoiselle Dee Dee. Now!" She motioned for everyone to leave and grabbed my hand for me to stay. Her grip was surprisingly tight and painful, like the pinch of a claw. Still I was not afraid of her, even though we would now be alone. She had screamed at my mother, and somehow, perversely, I liked that. It was a new sensation for me; it made me feel somehow stronger, more grown up. It was a sensation that would return to me from time to time in my young life, sometimes with similar glee and at other times with great shame. I had never questioned or faulted my mother before, and now I saw her anew, from afar, as other people might have seen her. Perhaps, I like to think, this even saved me, for I did not get caught up in her unexplained worries and fears. I waited on the old woman's bed before her miniature figure. She laughed hoarsely. "'Behold, the dreamer cometh.'" She looked me slowly up and down, smiled, waved at me with both hands as if I were some strange animal in the zoo, and made me laugh. She said, "You're a fine little boy. Yes, a little prince. Nothing to be ashamed of. Always take your sweet time when you need to. Time is your loyal servant. Don't let any of those women make you crazy. Women like to do that when they're not happy themselves. Though men are not much better." She tapped me with a hard fingernail on the forehead. "You have good *baxt*—that's the Gypsy word for fortune and luck. Remember that. You'll be fine, except your ears."

She cleared her throat as if she was going to tell me another mysterious secret, but then she began to cough. The cough became a hacking spasm, and she pulled a tasseled cord with a tiny trembling hand. Her maid and another young woman, a uniformed nurse, came rushing in from opposite ends of the room. The nurse joined us on the bed, scrambling on her hands and knees. She briskly pounded the old woman's tiny hunched back with her fists. The maid swooped me up in her arms, placed me upright on the floor, and led me away. As we went down the hallway, I could still hear the coughing behind the heavy closed door.

In the car back to Windsor, I felt something wet leaking out of my left ear. It was a liquid, thin and runny. I touched it and brought my finger to my nose. It had an unpleasant smell. It was pus. I held my finger up to my mother. My eardrum had perforated, though I did not know this at the time. I thought Berenice was talking louder than usual.

"Jeez, that woman gave me the heebie-jeebies. I'd never go back there again."

"You wouldn't be invited," Hannalore said.

"We better go directly to Dr. Desjarlais's office, Hannalore," my mother said.

And then I realized my hearing had improved.

Whatever the three women had hoped to accomplish by taking me to Grosse Pointe, it had a different and unexpected result. This effect was not at first apparent to anyone. My mother and Berenice were preoccupied with my new ear infection and the threat it might be to my hearing.

Dr. Desjarlais reassured my mother that the perforation was really quite small and actually helpful. "This is how the body tries to heal itself, by expelling the infection. Otherwise it could go straight into the boy's brain, and the jig would be up. I could tell you cases! We'll have to put him on penicillin for a while, just to be safe. But don't worry: the hole in the eardrum will close by itself."

In addition to the new and perverse sense of glee I had felt when the prophetess called my mother stupid, I now believed we were poor like the Israelite slaves in Egypt. Our house was no better than a shabby lean-to in the desert. I became obsessed with Hannalore. I had never given much thought to her. She had been a peripheral person in my life. A rare apparition. I now realized she was richer than I had ever imagined. How lucky she was! I became obsessed as well with all the other palaces we had passed that morning in Grosse Pointe. How wonderful, I thought, to have bedrooms as large as houses, each filled with beautiful treasures, to have marble floors with stars and flying horses, and stained-glass windows like those in our synagogue.

"Why can't we be rich like Hannalore and her friends?" I questioned my mother. At first I did not go so far as to actually say that it must be because my mother was stupid, though I was convinced this was the case. I scrutinized her actions, looking for clues and irrefutable proofs. I noted the confusion of spoons, knives, and forks in the kitchen drawers. I saw the disorder of papers, pens, and pencils on her telephone desk. In this new fixation, it did not occur to me to blame my father, our real breadwinner, for our poverty. I felt it was simply my mother's fault.

"Our house is so tiny. It fits in Hannalore's bedroom."

I realized that the bedroom I saw was Mademoiselle Dee Dee's, but I assumed Hannalore had a similar one in her palace.

"That was not Hannalore's bedroom, honey. Hannalore is just a servant, a maid like our Cathy."

Berenice chimed in, trying to defend the status of her sister-in-law. She addressed herself more to my mother than to me, with a slight irritation in her voice that I had never heard before: "Hannalore is *not* a servant or a maid; she is a well-trained, well-paid professional. She has her freedom to come and go. But she is not rich, either. She does not own any of those houses. Do you understand what I mean, Alexander? Her rooms are actually quite modest."

"But she has a convertible and lives in such a beautiful house and has a beautiful golden cross."

My mother became agitated. "What do you mean, a beautiful cross? Do you want to wear a necklace with a cross too? It's not normal for a rabbi's son to want to wear a cross!"

Berenice tried to calm her down. "Oh, Sarah, Sarah, he's only a child. He didn't say that. You're putting words in his mouth."

"Well, I guess I just don't know my own child."

The next afternoon my mother and Berenice attempted to show me different neighborhoods of Windsor, as a lesson in wealth and poverty. We drove by the poorest areas, where the houses were much smaller than ours and very run down. "See how lucky you are to live in your nice roomy house with your own bedroom?" Berenice said. "You even have your very own bathroom. That's quite a luxury for a kid. I never had my own when I was growing up. I had to share one with my parents and brother." Then we drove through the more wealthy areas, such as Walkerville, whose houses and streets, though stately, did not compare with the mansions of Grosse Pointe.

Berenice said, "Even the biggest palace in the world wouldn't make you any happier, Alexander. Only love makes people happy, and everyone loves you."

I sat in the backseat of the car with my arms folded and pretended not to see or hear anything. Try as they might, they could not dissuade me from my conviction of our poverty. Didn't the monkey-in-a-teacup woman say my mother was stupid? That women make you crazy when they're not happy themselves? How could I trust them?

This obsession or delusion went on for many days and resulted in my father's becoming aware of my visit to the prophetess. I went into his library and told him myself. "And women are stupid," I added.

He sighed. "Only foolish and bad things come from asking witches questions. That's why the Torah forbids it."

For a moment I became scared. Maybe Mademoiselle Dee Dee would come and get me, like the witches in the fairy tales that crept quietly after children, stealthily, the way witches creep.

"Is Mademoiselle Dee Dee really a witch?"

My father finally laughed. "Is that what old witches call themselves nowadays? Mademoiselle Dee Dee?" He smiled to reassure me, then shook his hands in the air, grimacing in mock fright. "Well, maybe she's not. *Nicht eine wirkliche Hexe.*

But still it's wrong. Since the Temple was destroyed, true prophecy has been weakened."

Immediately after this discussion, we came out of his library. My father gently asked me to go to my room. After he followed me to be sure that I obeyed, he went downstairs to speak with my mother. I heard him below, shutting the squeaky kitchen door.

Later, when I saw my mother in the living room, she looked tired and sad. I could not help myself. I will regret my words to my dying day, for one can never take away what has been spoken, as every spoken word is an eternal creation. Like God, we create and destroy our own world with words.

"We are stupid and poor!" I told my mother. "Stupid and poor, stupid and poor!"

She began to cry.

*T*here was finally no other option but to take me to see exactly where Hannalore lived. She came and picked me up in her car. That Sunday, the colder autumn weather had already begun. This time my mother and Berenice stayed home.

"I will take good care of our *petit prince,*" Hannalore said.

This outing had been carefully planned so as not to disturb the Fords or to backfire once again. Mr. Ford had recently remarried and had just left for Europe with his new wife and the daughters from his first marriage. Once inside the Ford estate, we parked in a small lot at the side of the great house, reserved for the servants and service people. Hannalore first took me on a tour of the house, proudly showing me through the enormous rooms, the grand hallways and vaulted galleries, pointing out imposing sculptures here, paintings by famous artists there. She appeared to forget the purpose of our visit. Hannalore was knowledgeable and intimate with many of these masterpieces. She commented on the various colors and pigments used on some of the oldest canvases.

"They made their paints themselves in those days, sometimes from ground stones, sometimes quite precious ones, and linseed oil. I once wanted to be a painter, but I had no ability." She expounded on the wealth of her employers, as if it were her own. "Well, we have to be so very rich to possess such treasures. We have some things here worth more than our house itself!"

Finally, almost reluctantly, Hannalore took me up to the servants' wing, to the attic apartment where she lived. She had modest, although not cramped, quarters. Her living room and bedroom had thick green wall-to-wall carpeting and gabled views of the formal gardens out back, where espaliered fruit trees clung to the perimeter walls. The trees looked so uncomfortable. I felt sorry for them, pressed up forever against their backs. Hannalore appeared to read my mind. "Poor things. They look like they, too, are being punished for our sins."

Hannalore's rooms had a musty air and were sparsely furnished. "I do not like clutter," she said. The furniture she did have looked comfortable enough but was not as nice as that which we had at home; certainly it did not share in any way the elegance or grandeur of the furnishings in the rest of the great house.

"So you see, *Alexandre*"—Hannalore sighed—"I am not so rich a person but a stranger in a rich man's house. I am really poorer than you. I am a simple, single working woman. Pitiful. But, *alors*, most of the world is not rich. It is a shame, but I shall die alone, far from my home."

When we were about to leave, Hannalore wanted to show off some more and leave through the grand foyer, exit down the front entrance, and then walk around the grounds to the back, where her car was parked.

In the grand foyer we came unexpectedly face-to-face with the most beautiful woman I had ever seen. The butler was standing behind her, removing a pale gray-blue fur coat. Another servant was carrying in heavy pieces of leather luggage.

This woman seemed to me too beautiful to be real. I blinked several times. She was young and thin, with abundant blond hair that fell around her shoulders. She shook her head after her coat was completely off and fluffed out her wonderful hair with her hands. She was totally unlike Hannalore, who appeared much older next to her, so bony and awkward.

This beautiful apparition was yet another species of woman, a species I had never encountered. Her skin was fine and clear. Her eyes were a piercing green. She was dressed in stretch pants and a turtleneck sweater of a shimmering light blue, a color that the old masters might have derived from the powder of lapis lazuli. This color, this ultramarine, itself seemed alive, a living, breathing thing, and moved with all the gentle curves of her body.

Though the woman was slightly shorter than Hannalore, her unexpected appearance produced an unsettling effect on her servant. Hannalore turned pale; she looked as if she might faint but quickly regained her composure. "Oh, Madame. How was your trip? Is everything all right, Madame? Madame is back so soon?"

Without saying a word, the woman looked inquisitively at me and then at Hannalore. Hannalore quickly improvised: "This is my nephew, Alexander. Say hello to Mrs. Ford."

Mrs. Ford smiled and extended a bejeweled hand. She smelled faintly of roses. "Hallo, I am Cristina." Her voice was loud. She too had an accent, but it was different from Hannalore's and the Cantor's. She then turned away, forgetting all about me, and spoke to Hannalore in a great rush of words. "Hannah . . . I mean, of course, Hannalore." She touched her arm lightly in apology. "Please, it is not my business, forgive me, but could you take that thing off just for now, or hide it under your collar." She touched Hannalore's little crucifix. "It upsets—how do you say?—my *nerves*. Haven't you heard? We have been excommunicated for our marriage!"

Then the woman turned to me again, bent forward ever so slightly, and smiled. She spoke slowly again. "And are you a sweet *leetle* boy?" The way she said *"leetle"* made me laugh out loud. She laughed too. *"Che bello!"* She patted my head, waved, then spun around and, like an exotic, wondrous bird, took flight, disappearing up the marble staircase.

Hannalore was sullen during the whole drive back to Windsor and did not address a word to me. Although the afternoon became colder still, she kept the top of her convertible down, as if she were overheated or could not get enough air. She smoked one cigarette after another while she drove, throwing the butts over the front windshield. One butt flew back into the car and hit me in the face. Hannalore muttered to herself in French and German, though I couldn't make out what she was saying. She kept touching her hair and the little gold crucifix on her neck and the belt around her waist. I am certain, when I recall this episode so many years later, although I did not know what it meant at the time, that she crossed herself two or three times, smoking cigarette in hand.

For the first time, after seeing such a beautiful woman, I had noticed Hannalore's looks in a critical way. Despite the powdery makeup Hannalore always wore, and her pink lipstick, her features were harsh, her skin sagged under her chin, her cheeks were finely wrinkled. The way she wore her slack white hair, curled just at the edges, flapping now in the open wind as she drove, seemed completely ridiculous. She is ugly, I thought. Ugly. Ugly. Ugly. And, I said to myself, she's not like me: she has no *baxt*.

When we arrived at my house we were greeted by my mother and Berenice. Hannalore pushed me forward and sighed. "It is *so* fortunate that our *petit prince* is so pretty, otherwise who knows if I would have angered the new Madame. *Die Italienerin* might not like strangers in her house. For me it could have meant the end." She raised her right forefinger and in a gruesome gesture sliced a red-lacquered fingernail across her neck.

Fluvius Regum

*D*uring my entire childhood and beyond, up until the day he died, my father worked on his magnum opus, or what he sometimes referred to half jokingly as "my sandstone ziggurat."

Although he intended his great work to be a vast trilogy, focusing on and encompassing in turn the three obscure themes that consumed him during his life, he managed to produce only half a dozen or so articles for esoteric, albeit highly respected, publications, like the *Royal Journal for Near Asiatic Studies* and the *Archiv für Semetische Sprachen*.

He made only limited headway in his first book, the

title of which was constantly changing, becoming more and more unwieldy over the years, while the ever elusive text itself seemed to diminish and contract: *The Academies on the Ancient Rivers of the East;* or *The Eternal Flux of Time: The Tigris and Euphrates;* or *Babylonia: The Shape and Paradigm of Dispersion and Exile.*

My father, in part, inherited his great passion for that area of the world from his grandfather. At the end of the last century, my great-grandfather, an amateur linguist and rare-book dealer, left his family and home in Frankfurt to travel as tutor to an exiled Persian prince. His journey lasted three years, and from the brief contact I had with his daughter, my grandmother, this expedition left a bitter aftertaste in his temporarily abandoned family. Together my great-grandfather and the prince visited what was once ancient Mesopotamia. My father sometimes told me stories he had heard as a child from his grandfather, heavily borrowed from *The Thousand and One Nights* and filled with flying carpets, adventurous boys, and djinns in bottles.

Upon my great-grandfather's return to Germany, he published a brief account of his expedition and adventures with the prince. My father kept this slender book prominently displayed on one of his library shelves, protected in a rectangular glass case that my great-grandfather himself had had specially made, a small transparent sarcophagus with its own little hinged door and miniature silver lock.

Next to it, in a small velvet jewelry box, lay a tiny silver key. The clumsy title on the book's leather cover was embossed in gold in the old-fashioned Gothic script: *Auf den Spuren Abrahams entlang des Euphrat.*

My father's duties to his congregation, his visits to the sick, his appointments with parishioners, the endless procession of weddings, births, and funerals, "the dizzying circle of life," as he called it, took up most of his time. When he was finished for the day or had time to spare, he would go into his library, which occupied a fair-size room on the second floor of our house. In the corner was a small bay window with a narrow bench, which jutted out over our backyard. Because of this window's wooden latticework, my father called it "the birdcage." When growing up in Toronto, he had heard how the Frankfurt people had porches, *Geräms*, with similar wooden latticework projecting out onto the streets. These structures were also called *Vogelbauern*, birdcages. On mild days neighbors might sit and read or gossip with each other, and the private life of the bourgeois home was thereby extended into the *freie Luft*—the out-of-doors.

I often sat in the birdcage and played by myself while he worked. From there I had a view of an enormous elm that stood in the corner of our backyard. My father named her the Great Goddess Asherah. Her divine canopy protected our house and back lawn in the years before the Dutch disease came to Windsor and all the dead and dying elms, this proud deity among them, were cut down. At the peak of her autumn foliage my father would say, "The Great Goddess Asherah is in her glory," or on a windy night, he might look out a window and proclaim, "The Goddess Asherah is singing a lonely song." Once he had explained in a sermon: "We must not think of the ancients who worshiped inanimate things, like trees, the oceans, or the sun, as fools; more likely they were wiser than we. They were astonished and lured by the natural world, in which they lived in closer harmony. Rather we are the greater fools with our own nowadays idols—Greed, Desire, Arrogance. We must struggle continuously to expel these destructive gods that dwell in our hearts."

At my father's library desk he would pore over various volumes, large and small, in Hebrew and Aramaic, in German and English. He would mark the innumerable places he found of interest, and to which he wished to return, with strips of brightly colored paper that stuck out their carnival heads from between the pages of his books.

In his library my father had the complete facsimiles of the Ugaritic tablets found by the French at Ras Shamra and the renowned transcriptions of C. H. Gordon in his *Ugaritic Handbook*. Some of his books he had inherited from his grandfather. His library also contained encyclopedias and extensive works of world literature and modern science, the latter including many texts on physics and mathematics. My father had earned a master's degree in physics before choosing to become a rabbi, a decision that was a grave disappointment to his atheistic and secularly academic parents. It was one of two factors contributing to the painful and long-standing rift between the two generations, a rift that as a child I was only vaguely aware of and whose second major component I did not yet understand.

My father called the pure sciences "the fascinating but cold religions of the north" and always said he preferred "the warmth of the Torah and"—though he had never himself visited them—"the sunny lands of its birth."

When he sat down to work, my father would leaf through his catalogue of notebooks, some already showing signs of age, adding a few paragraphs here, a footnote there. Often he read through the extensive correspondence he had maintained with famous scholars around the world.

On one wall of his study was a vast map of Babylonia during the time of the Talmud. The courses of the Tigris and Euphrates were drawn in jagged lines. They diverged, converged, and diverged again. The Tigris zigzagged to the Great Gulf in a deep waxy red, the Euphrates in cobalt blue. To this day I associate these colors, appearing as they always do in the most unexpected places—in a bowl of artificial fruit or scattered in a reproduction of a Florentine mural—with those faraway and mighty streams. I yearned to see the great rivers flow straight and smooth, rather than old and wrinkled as they appeared to me then. Sometimes I would try crossing my eyes, but this resulted only in the two rivers becoming four, crisscrossing each other in parts, blue over red, red over blue. I could never make them parallel or merge them into one.

My father explained that the Euphrates had its source in *Gan Ayden*, the Garden of Eden, and he enumerated the other three rivers in the Bible that originated there as well: Pishon, which compasses the whole land of Havila, where there is gold and bdellium and the Shoham stone; and Gihon, which compasses the whole land of Kush; and the third river, the Hiddeqel, which flows toward the east of the city Ashshur and which many say is the Tigris.

On the great map there were canals to be reckoned with too, connecting the two rivers and, between them, irrigating a fertile swath; these channels included the Fluvius Regum, the Royal River, where the cities of Nehardea and Mahuza lay at opposite ends; the Nahar Shinvattah, upon whose banks Pumbedita lay; and the Nahar Sura, where the city of the same name crouched in waiting for its turn of scholarly fame. On my father's map these academic centers, Sura Pumbedita, Nehardea, and Mahuza, along with others of lesser renown, were tagged with colored flag pins. One day my father might receive a letter from a scholar in Jerusalem or London or Cape Town and, as if needing a witness for the momentous event that was taking place, would call me into his room as he adjusted his map according to the information his colleague had conveyed, moving a colored flag a slight distance here or there along the jagged course of the Euphrates, or from one bank of the Fluvius Regum to the other. Sometimes a river itself needed to be adjusted, as the courses of rivers changed over the millennia. Modern maps did not always reflect the ancient pathways. In the days of the Patriarchs, my father told me, the Tigris and the Euphrates had separate mouths on the Gulf.

A major beneficiary of my father's international correspondence was my stamp collection. One day he was about to show me how to cut off the corners of the envelopes and soak them in water to remove their philatelic treasures. Instead I asked my father to save the envelopes whole. My father was delighted at my idea and thought it amazing that a young boy would have such foresight, another sign of uncommon intellect in a child who had quickly learned to read two alphabets and was acquiring three languages.

"Not only will you have a fine collection of stamps," he told me, "but a fine collection of scholars' handwriting." Then he said, "Alexander, do you know who are more powerful, scholars or kings?" Without waiting, he answered the question himself. "Scholars. Because they have the power to change the way people think."

I sometimes believe the impression I made on him with the envelopes is the reason he never shared my mother's early worries about me, though I cannot recall him in those early days ever challenging her or defending me in her presence, except to say reassuringly, as others had, "Well, Sarah, he's only a child." I suspect he spoke to her privately about me, out of my hearing, more forcefully, though still in his own calm way, no doubt from a tender respect for my mother's feelings and concerns. But the most important result of this profound impression I made on him, the most significant benefit to me, I believe, was the quiet and stubborn way he protected me from the ominous course of treatments that my mother proposed many years later.

The simple truth, when I asked to preserve the envelopes, had nothing to do with an admiration for scholars. The envelopes themselves fascinated me, and they fascinated me more than their various stamps with dour faces of queens, kings, and prime ministers. They delighted me with their promise of exotic places where real people lived in the nowadays, with their foreign shapes and textures, and their varied and odd scripts, some slanting this way, others that, spelling out their names and my father's. Didn't my father's name contain part of my own, and mine part of his? I loved the faint musty scent of the material they were made of. For the most part these ambassadors from afar were light and translucent, sometimes a creamy white or more often a pale blue, unlike the insistent cobalt of the Euphrates on my father's wall. I could hold them up to the light of a window and see the random fibrous skeleton of the paper, or see my fingers on the other side, transilluminated by a universally shining sun.

Whenever my father repositioned the cities on his map, or the courses of the rivers and canals, he would say, "Alexander, I like to get my coordinates exactly right. It's human nature to seek out patterns wherever they may present themselves." And he would always add, saying the big words slowly, as if this would make me understand: "This seeking after patterns is nothing more than man's natural yearning to know God. It underlies every pursuit of knowledge."

In my father's case, I believe, it was indeed so. My father's interest in the patterns of those ancient rivers and canals, and the long vanished cities and academies on their banks, was somehow tied in with his other lifelong fascination, the intended theme of the second volume of his magnum opus, the theosophical study of the shape of the Godhead. By this shape I refer to the elaborate structure of the Divine Being Himself as deduced by ancient mystics seeking to understand the relationship of a nonphysical God to His physical creation. In these theories, it is through the ten emanations of divine power, the so-called Holy Sefirot, that God comes forth from His infinite, unknowable being and manifests Himself in Creation.

In a small glass-and-wood frame, on another wall of my father's library, was a rare beige incunabulum with pigments of gold, green, ruby, and purple, a page from an ancient text, on which was depicted a diagram of the symbolic Sefirotic Tree. The great sphere-shaped potencies of God, those emanations of His divine power, hung symmetrically and heavily from its branches like oversized mutant fruits: a grand balancing act that appeared to prevent the tree, and the known universe it represented, from tumbling over; the weight of Understanding held its own opposite Wisdom, the harshness of Law opposite Loving-kindness, Splendor against Eternity. The trunk itself was composed of Kingdom, Foundation, and Glory. At the very top was the gold and palmate Crown. Sometimes I would gaze across the room from the narrow bench of the birdcage, contemplating the colors of the massive fruit. This would send me into a long reverie. I would see myself alighting in the form of a dove or a sparrow onto one of the tree's branches and, from the imperceptible flutter of my wings and the weight of my feathers, toppling it over. Then I would fly out, a creature without physical density or mass, through the solid book-lined walls of the library, to the Goddess Asherah. From her branches I'd look back at the small child sitting alone inside the glassy cage of the bay window, and I would wonder at the mystery of being two things at once, a magic little bird moving through the air and a solitary, daydreaming boy.

On some of these occasions my mother might come

and stand in the doorway of the study. I would pretend I didn't see her. She'd ask my father with concern, "Why don't you tell him to play outside for a while? He's just sitting there staring."

"Oh, he's all right, Sarah. Children do that."

But then, in order to reassure my mother, he would say, "Alexander, your mother is right. It's a beautiful day. Why don't you go outside and get some fresh air?"

And I would go outside and play alone beneath the shade of the Great Goddess Asherah.

Nowadays, so many years later, when I look at the picture of the Sefirotic Tree, I am filled with sorrow. I believe that as my father grew older, his speculations and delvings confused him and hindered him more and more in his work and his world. And they inadvertently caused a terrible rift, a fatal distance, between him and my mother.

St. Thomas

One day I came home from school, to find my father covering all the mirrors in the house with sheets. That was when I first learned that my mother had a brother—that I had an uncle.

My father spoke in an uncharacteristic, awkward tone, as if he had been practicing a new language and was mindful of making mistakes.

"Your mother's brother died, your uncle Avner. You never met him. He was sick for a long time." Then he paused, weighing his words. I believe to this day that he was under some constraint of my mother's, some command he dared not openly break, though he could not help fighting with himself.

"Avner was in the hospital at St. Thomas. That's why you never met him. We just heard, and your mother rushed up to Toronto for the funeral. She'll come home late tonight on the train if she's not too tired."

At first, when my father said, "sick for a long time," I imagined this meant my unknown uncle had some physical ailment, like my ear infections that Dr. Desjarlais said could go straight into the brain. But when my father paused and mentioned St. Thomas, I felt a chill up my spine. St. Thomas was a place for crazy people, a place I believed no one ever came back from. In Windsor, people would say when seeing someone talk to himself on the street, "He belongs in St. Thomas."

Once, for several weeks, someone went around Windsor killing dogs. People would wake up in the morning to find their beloved pets strangled, hanging from a tree or a fence post in their backyards. The eyes were always gouged out, the bloody orbs hanging from their sockets on stringy white nerves. Their genitalia would be cut off and lying nearby on the ground. The most famous woman in Windsor, Eva Moore, the television hostess of the *Sunday Afternoon Movie*, broadcast an impassioned appeal to the citizens of the city. Holding her dachshund, Bijou, this otherwise elegant and serene lady said tearfully, "Until this evil Satan is found, the Prince of Puppies and I shall not sleep!"

The perpetrator, an adolescent boy from the nearby town of Belle River, was finally apprehended. The blazing red headlines in the *Star* read: "Deranged Youth Caught. Committed to St. Thomas for Unnatural Crimes." When I remembered this I shuddered. I wanted to ask my father, "Did Uncle Avner kill dogs? Did he cut off their private parts and leave them on the ground?" Instead I asked, "Did Grandma and Grandpa go to the funeral?" I rarely saw my mother's parents, and never my father's. My father's parents had moved back to Frankfurt the year I was born.

My father seemed surprised by this question. "Of course, Alexander. Avner was their son. Parents love their children no matter what they're like. It's human nature. Someday, hopefully, you'll understand that too." I was only eight or nine at the time, and this word "hopefully," as my father tentatively said it—for it was the only time that I sensed doubt in his voice—filled me with a sense of dread. Then my father said, "I'll make dinner. Actually that's a bit of an exaggeration. The Cantor cooked us something great. His *Confit Alexandre*, with garlic and allspice! I just have to warm it in the oven for fifteen minutes. And there's also grilled potatoes and a salad. Berenice brought everything over." My father made a dramatic gesture with his arm. "'She is like the merchant ships; she brings her food from afar!'"

I had no appetite for dinner, even the gourmet one the Cantor had cooked and Berenice had brought over, but I forced myself to eat anyway. The glazed thigh of the duck smelled putrid, the small potatoes tasted rubbery. I ate slowly. My father was talking the whole time, something about the siege of Mahuza, and a letter he received from his colleague Dr. Aschenbach in Brooklyn, New York, who was an expert on the subject. "It's amazing that he can find out information that's been thought to be lost for over a thousand years."

I did not pay much attention to anything my father said, to the actual information that Dr. Aschenbach had retrieved from over a thousand years before. I could not stop thinking of the boy who tortured all those dogs, popping out their eyeballs, cutting into the soft meat of their private parts.

I suddenly excused myself. I ran upstairs to my bathroom. I locked the door so my father wouldn't hear me and vomited my entire dinner into the toilet bowl. I brushed my teeth. I scrubbed the pink insides of my mouth over and over until I spat blood in the sink.

When my mother returned late that night, I was in my bedroom, supposedly asleep. I slipped out and hid near the upstairs banister. My mother walked briskly into the house with my father. He had picked her up at the station. She made my father take down all the sheets on the mirrors.

"Do it right now, please," she said. "I won't be sitting shiva."

"But your brother died." My father sounded perplexed.

"I won't be sitting shiva," she repeated, this time with an irritated tone. "For what? I really just can't. God forgive me. The Avner I knew and loved died a long time ago. Even your parents couldn't bear knowing I had such a brother. It made them flee this country."

"It never made any difference to me, Sarah. I didn't listen to them. I married you, didn't I?"

"That was very kind of you, under the circumstances."

"Well, it's very sad, Sarah. Very sad. Poor sweet Avner."

"And you know I was only a little girl when they put Avner away."

"I know that, Sarah. I know."

"How could I have stopped them? . . . What could I have done?"

"No one is blaming you, Sarah. No one. You were only a child. It was God's will. Why do you always blame yourself?"

Even without seeing him, I knew my father was mournfully shaking his head.

A short while later, my mother came up to my room and sat very gently at the foot of my bed. I now pretended I was waking from a deep slumber.

"Go back to sleep, sweetheart, go back to sleep," my mother said as she got up to leave. She bent over and kissed me on the forehead. "I just wanted to see if you were all right."

Strasbourg /
Straßburg

*T*he Cantor and his sister Hannalore grew up in the border city of Strasbourg, France. This accounted for their fluency in both French and German, as well as the Alsatian dialect.

"We lived in the center of town," Hannalore once explained, "an island between two arms of the same river, the Ill River. An island shaped like a kiss." She puckered her thin red-colored lips, making them seem fuller, oval. "Like so."

We all laughed.

"*C'est vrai!*" she said. "Am I a liar, Bernhard? *Bin ich eine Lügnerin?* Tell them."

Her brother agreed. *"C'est vrai, Hannalore, c'est vrai."*

"I was born on an island too!" Berenice added.

Berenice grew up on the island of Montreal but came from an English-speaking community, Outremont, and so she understood and spoke only an occasional and halting French. Sometimes, when she said something in her bad Quebecois, the Cantor and Hannalore gently made fun of her. "Your accent, Madame Berenice . . . ," they would say, slowly, so as to draw out their little jest. "Are you from the Ivory Coast? Oh, perhaps Belgium? Oh, are you from Romania? No? Of course! From Paris!" And the Cantor and Hannalore would burst into laughter, along with good-natured Berenice. My parents would just smile politely. They did not believe in embarrassing anyone, although Berenice never seemed embarrassed, and my mother and father could not tell at all the difference between any two French accents.

Sometimes my mother would make a show of patting Berenice's hand, coming publicly to her defense. "I wish I knew as much French as Berenice. I know about ten words. And she reads it so well too. When we go shopping, she can read every label—"

And this would start them all laughing again. *"Madame Rabbi,"* the Cantor and Hannalore would say in chorus, *"tu es adorable!"*

My mother would turn crimson.

Finally the Cantor and Hannalore would smile and slip into Alsatian, a show of great affection after all their teasing, for it seemed to me that they spoke their home dialect only at moments of great intimacy. "Berenice, Berenice, *redd wie d'r de schnawel gewachse isch!* Just speak the way your beak grew!"

As a young teenager, the Cantor had left the Rue des Frères on the island shaped like a kiss where he and Hannalore had grown up. He went off to Paris to study voice and music in a conservatory. "If it weren't for the terrible war," Berenice would always say, "he probably would have had an opera career; his voice is *that* good. Sometimes you can fall in love with a part of a person that isn't even a bodily part, merely a projection of themselves that wanders out into the world, like their voice or their personality, but then you come to know and love the whole physical person. The original source." And she would always add, returning to her subject, "But he is very happy as a cantor. He has no regrets."

The Cantor's body was tall and thin, exactly like his twin sister Hannalore's, but his face was plump and the skin very soft and smooth. He was four or five years older than Berenice. He was a composer, too, and wrote his own music for services. I especially loved his "Happy Are Those" and "Come and Greet the Sabbath Bride." And later, when it was too late, long after I first heard it, I would come to

love more than anything else, to love unbearably, his irre-
trievable, once-in-a-lifetime melody, "Praise Him Sun and
Moon, Praise Him All You Stars of Light."

Berenice would always report to my mother and me on
the Cantor's current project. Unlike my father, who closed
himself in his study upstairs, the Cantor would walk
through his house and sing *sotto voce* until he figured out the
exact melody. Then he would sit at the spinet in the living
room and write out his score on pale-blue music paper. The
notes and chords ran across the page, lightly, like the
toeprints of sparrows.

Sometimes when I came over to their house the Cantor
would begin playing Poulenc's "Le Lion amoureux," on account of my Hebrew name. Berenice would come hurrying
into the living room from the kitchen or the backyard or
wherever she had been. "Come here, let's dance, Aryeh!"
These were the only times she referred to me by my Hebrew name. Then we would waltz a little through the living
room, Berenice whirling around me while the Cantor
played.

It more than once occurred to me that when God created the real lions, He likewise spoke my name, and perhaps His speech, the true *Ursprache* and the matrix of all
language, was more like this enchanting, welcoming music
than words.

Somehow the music itself did not seem to me to match
the story Berenice had told me about the poor lovesick lion

who was persuaded to let his claws and teeth be removed so he could marry his sweetheart. After he submitted to this degradation, he was cruelly rejected.

"Some of those fables are so mean," Berenice said. "And those gruesome German tales your dear father reads to you are even worse! Witches trying to cook children! Yuck! Really I don't understand him. Such a beautiful and sensitive man!"

Besides composing, the Cantor had another interest, the greenhouse that he designed and built in his backyard. The glass structure stood nearly as high as the house, almost two stories, but was no more than ten or twelve feet deep. Throughout the cool and cold months it was humid and warm inside. With my fingertips I could draw figures on the misty panes. The Cantor called it the Palmenhaus, and in it grew several species of palm. When I was still a child he had at least a dozen small trees in various large clay pots, which stood on low platforms with casters. None of the trees were much taller than the adults I knew.

In the beginning of June, when the warm weather was reliable, he took the palms out of the greenhouse and placed them in a circle on the patio. Later in the summer, when we went to our cottages, he loaded them on a truck, which he rented for this purpose. At the lake they stood on a small tiled terrace the Cantor had laid out on an embankment overlooking the beach. "The fresh air will do them good."

The Cantor expected his beloved trees to reach great heights.

"One day they will no longer fit back in the Palmenhaus," he said.

"What will you do then?" I asked.

"I will send them to the Sorbonne to be educated." He looked at me with his gray eyes. "Or maybe, someday, someone will build them a bigger greenhouse."

Once I overheard Berenice confide to my mother that sometimes the Cantor paid more attention to his palms than to her, even referring to them as his children. "He has names for each one," she said.

Later I went up to him and asked what their names were.

He looked at me, surprised. "What names?"

"The palm trees that have children's names."

His face turned red, then he seemed very sad. "Has Aunt Berenice been chattering again?" I think he realized that his sad look had unsettled me, and so he smiled with an extreme effort and patted my head. "Yes, of course. Berenice is right, Alexander, but confused. They have names, but Latin names, scientific names, not people names, of course."

And he began listing them on his fingers: "*Metroxylon, Nifpa fruticans, Arenga pinnata* . . ." Then he stopped himself and said, "No, *mein Löwe*, I will tell you a secret, but only to you. It is true, they do have names, but of famous characters, imaginary and real: Tosca, Caravaggio, Richard Tauber, Lotte Lehmann. Tauber and Lehmann are favorite singers of mine. Come inside and I will play something for you."

This was one of the few moments in my life that I remember being all alone with the Cantor, without Berenice or my parents around. Somehow this made me feel very grown up. I was proud the Cantor was giving me his complete attention, that he was somehow confiding in me. In the living room, the Cantor took a seventy-eight from its sleeve and put it on the phonograph.

"Listen to this carefully, Aryeh Alexander. The recording is old and scratchy. I fell in love with this song when I first heard it after the war. And when I first met Berenice I fell in love with her too, because she reminded me of it."

The music began, and the German tenor Richard Tauber sang longingly, in a heavily accented English, the language of his exile.

> *Sylvia's hair is like the night,*
> *touched with glancing starry beams,*
> *such a face as drifts through dreams—*
> *this is Sylvia to the sight.*

I had a strange feeling, listening to this song. Though I loved Berenice, I could not think of her in this romantic way, the way the Cantor somehow did, with starry beams upon her hair or a face that drifted through dreams.

When the record was over I saw that the Cantor was sitting in his chair, looking out a window, his eyes moist. He was very quiet and seemed to have forgotten I was there.

I pretended I had become invisible, and slowly, silently, I left the living room and their house.

Tecumseh Road

When I was still in elementary school, a little boy and girl from a nearby neighborhood were killed. Their parents belonged to my father's congregation, and my mother had taught both children in the synagogue's afternoon kindergarten. The girl, who was six, and the boy, who was five, were playing in their backyard on a corner lot a few blocks from our house. A car lost control and drove through their green picket fence and ran them both over. The girl was dragged over thirty feet and decapitated. The boy died an hour after his sister in Hôtel-Dieu, from internal injuries. It happened on a Saturday morning and the same day was in a special afternoon edition of the paper in large red letters: TWO CHILDREN KILLED ON TECUMSEH ROAD.

When my mother picked up the paper and saw the headline and a picture of the children in happier days, she immediately started crying. A few moments after the newspapers were delivered, Berenice came running over to our porch, and the two friends fell into each other's arms.

Later that same afternoon the distraught parents came to our house to talk to my father. When the parents walked into our house, I recognized their faces because they occasionally came to synagogue. But here in our living room they were different, like ghosts or the walking dead. I hid behind the china cabinet while my father slowly and gently asked them questions in preparation for the double funeral.

"What was your little girl's Hebrew name? What was the little boy's name? When were they each born?"

Each question and answer was interrupted by terrible cries from the mother, which were mixed with the continuous weeping of my own mother, whom I spied holding her stomach as if in great pain. Somehow my mother suddenly sensed I was in the room and came over to me in my hiding place. She knew I had developed the habit of eavesdropping. At first she did not say a word. She could not speak, her face, her mouth and eyes, were so distorted by grief. Finally she made herself whisper. The words came out in little gasps. "Alexander, how . . . could . . . you? How . . . can . . . you laugh?"

"I wasn't laughing."

I did not mean to lie but was unable to explain to my mother that I could not help myself, that I laughed because I was afraid, even though I did not know why. It did not consciously occur to me to be afraid that I myself could be run over and decapitated while playing in my backyard or on the street.

My mother weakly pointed the way upstairs. At first I obeyed and went to my room; but even there I could hear the terrible cries of the mother of the dead children, which were mixed with those of my own mother.

I slipped down the stairs and out of the house. I walked over to Tecumseh Road. I knew where I was going but pretended I did not know. I imagined I was under remote control, perhaps by aliens, or, as I continued to walk further, enchanted by the spell of a witch. I was not responsible for my actions. They were not as they appeared to be. And I could not even say what form I myself took. Perhaps I had become a baby deer or a tiny toad or had acquired the feathery skin of a swan. I allowed myself to be taken over by these magical forces. I walked mechanically and then stopped. I stood and watched from almost a block away, because other voyeurs had crowded around the sidewalk near the corner yard. From my vantage point I saw the picket fence that had been knocked over and the muddy brown ruts in the green lawn where the car had skidded to its fatal stop near the back porch.

A woman came over to me and slapped me across the face. "Shame on you! Shame! What are you doing? What are you doing here? What is your name? Who are your parents?" I did not answer her. I could not. The forces had now turned me into a solemn and grim statue. I waited a long while until she walked away.

After the woman left I sensed someone's sour breath on my neck. It was the gentile girl who used to come with her mother to hear the Cantor sing in synagogue. I had not seen her in two or three years. I had never seen her up close before. She and her mother had always sat in the last row of the women's section and left before services were over.

The girl's arms and legs were like sticks and her back was twisted. She was dressed in a purple velvet dress, as if she was going to a party. She wore a brilliant gold necklace studded with green and red jewels, which seemed too heavy for such a skinny girl. She walked around me like an ungainly but exotic bird, looking at me with first one eye and then the other. Her center of gravity seemed to shift with each step. Now it was in one of her stick legs, now in the middle of her scrawny stomach, now in her chin, which jutted forward. I was surprised she didn't tip over.

She had a peculiar voice, high-pitched and nasal.

"I just got here this instant. I called a taxi as soon as I saw the newspaper. We keep an account with Checker. I almost missed seeing the paper because I was just about to call my dear personal friend Miss Eva Moore and go over for a visit. We've been meaning to get together for a long time, but the headlines caught my eye. Been here long?" The girl stopped talking for a long moment to catch her breath. "I think it's hilarious too. My mother said those children had to die because of their parents' sins. Certainly not their own. Though, of course, Mother says it's so unfair. They were too young to have their own mortal sins. I wonder what the parents *did*. It must have been god-awful. They must have poked their private things where they shouldn't have. But you have to take my mother with a grain of salt. I certainly do. Frankly I think those kids just died because they didn't look both ways!" She started laughing at her own joke, part snorting, part choking. She stared closely in my face. Her hair was short and curly; it looked brownish and brittle, as if it might all suddenly fall off. She was wearing lipstick and eye shadow although she did not seem older than ten or eleven. I was still standing grim and silent like a statue.

"Well, cat got your tongue? Now you're all stiff and serious. Are you Lot's wife? She turned to a pillar of salt because she looked when she wasn't supposed to. Were you looking at something you were told not to? Something dirty? Do you ever touch yourself? Are you afraid of me? I think you're afraid of me because I'm deformed. I remind you of death."

I stopped being a grim statue and looked back at her.

"I'm not afraid of you."

"You're embarrassed. You're turning red."

"I'm not embarrassed."

"Suit yourself. My name is Marla Cook, and I have to be on my way. I've seen what I came to see. Mission accomplished. Big deal. 'Death be not proud!' Blah, blah. I don't have much energy to chat or recite poetry." She started walking away. A taxi was waiting for her on the corner. She stopped and came back toward me.

"I have a hole in my heart and could die at any time. Just like those stupid kids. I'm going to have to go to Texas for another operation because they're too stupid to do them in Toronto. I've had three already. Good-bye, Mrs. Lot." Then she told me her address. She lived in the wealthy neighborhood of Walkerville.

The next day, after my parents returned from the children's funeral, my mother said she did not feel well. "I think I need to go to the hospital."

My father took her to Hôtel-Dieu.

"Mother needs to get her strength back," my father said

when he came home that evening. "She is so sensitive to things, it affects her physically."

I must have looked frightened, because my father put his hand on my shoulder and said, "Don't worry, Alexander. Mother will get better soon. She always does."

And several days later she came home.

Britannia

When I was ten my mother told me she was pregnant.

"You know, Alexander, I'm already beginning my fourth month."

I was glad to hear this news, although I had never felt lonely for brothers and sisters. I had occasionally felt an undefined loneliness, but as I have already mentioned, it was not for the company of other children. Immediately I wondered about the shimmering name announced in heaven that was bringing forth this new soul.

At first my mother did not look particularly different to

me. There was only a small bulge in her belly, and beside her brief but happy announcement, I learned little about her situation. The actual details, the ups and downs of my parents' attempts to have another child, I soon heard from Berenice. My mother had, excepting her very first pregnancy, with me, conceived several times but always lost the baby in the first weeks. Berenice explained to me: "You know, Alexander, your mother's been trying again for a long time, but the opening to her womb is too loose. Just like a trapdoor. You must have been clever to hold the door shut the whole time. I always imagine you in there alert, using all your strength to stay in until you were ready to come out. That's one of the reasons why I think you must be pretty smart and strong. A real survivor, to have figured it all out *before* you were born!"

Years later, when I was changing inside, I began to dream I was locked in a dark space, holding the door shut with all my strength while vicious dogs or monsters waited outside to get me. The oxygen would start to run out, and I would wake drenched in sweat, gasping for air. But back then when I was ten and Berenice made her revelation, I calmly realized that the times over the years when my mother had not felt well or on the rare occasions when she had to go for a few days to the hospital for a "checkup" were in fact the times of her miscarriages. I thought of all my brothers and sisters who had died terrible deaths, dragged from one terrible darkness into another, like the little girl and boy who were dragged into the darkness as they played in their backyard on Tecumseh Road.

The announcement of her pregnancy happened late in the spring, and I cannot remember my mother ever being so happy. Although she was still a young woman, she began to seem even younger, her skin smoother, her features softer. I began to love her intensely at this time and wanted to stay close to her and join in her happiness. For her part she could hardly believe that after ten years she might merit another child. She was excited to share the news with me. I could tell this when she said, "You know, Alexander, I'm already beginning my fourth month." Yet her happiness was colored by a great fear of losing the baby. She submitted without complaint to the doctor's strict orders, which confined her to bed until the end of her pregnancy.

"I won't be able to be such a good mom for the next few months, Alexander. I hope you won't mind too much. You know I love you. Berenice said she would help out. I can't thank her enough. I won't be able to go to the lake this summer, so Berenice and the Cantor will take you. I need to be near the hospital, just in case. Your father can use his vacation to stay home and work on his book and take care of me."

I was, of course, very disappointed that I would be away from my parents the whole summer, especially my mother, when I had grown to love her so greatly during this time of her rejuvenation. I regretted any unhappiness or worry I might have caused her. I realized I had a stubborn heart, especially when I'd tormented her just a few years before with my complaint "We are stupid and poor! Stupid and poor!" and made her cry. Sometimes this made me feel so bad I began telling myself that I had really said, "Smart and rich! Smart and rich!" And that my mother had laughed a wonderful laugh and hugged me in her arms the way Berenice always did and answered, "Yes, we are, sweetheart, yes we are. Smart and rich. Smart and rich." Then the thought that by substituting one phrase for the other, and repeating it over and over in my mind, I might change what happened in the past would occur to me as being completely irrational. But I could not help myself, and sometimes I would lie awake late at night repeating, "We are smart and rich. We are smart and rich," until I finally exhausted myself and fell asleep.

My mother sensed my sadness at the prospect of being separated from her. She tried to reassure me. "Of course, Berenice and the Cantor will bring you back every other week if you want to visit or are homesick. You know it's only a half hour to Belle River. You don't even have to go if you don't want to, but it will be healthy for you to be at the lake, and Berenice has planned some lovely outings. She would be very disappointed. You are very important to her. She loves you so much, almost as much as I do."

My mother then told me a story I had heard once before but had forgotten. One summer when I was a toddler I had wandered into the lake, wading in the shallows up to my little chest. "We never thought you could walk so far yet—you had just started! Berenice saw a small wave coming toward you that in another instant would have drowned you. She ran into the water and drew you out just like Pharaoh's daughter—your father and I even called her that for a long time. Pharaoh's Daughter. It sounds so beautiful. After that I learned my lesson and always kept you directly in sight."

Then my mother said something that has haunted me my whole life, though I do not clearly know why: "Maybe because I've let Berenice share you, God will bless me with another child."

*T*he beginning of my mother's confinement coincided with a historic event in southern Ontario: the Queen's visit to Canada on the royal yacht *Britannia*. The whole southern province was excited, but especially Windsor, where Her Majesty was scheduled to make an overnight stop. For weeks before her arrival the local paper was full of articles and maps describing the route the *Britannia* would take. I also read about the ship's interior: the royal bedroom suites; the family sitting room, which, although grand in size, was still as cozy and comfortable as any commoner's living room; and the magnificent dining room, with tables for sixty guests.

I studied the scheduled route of the splendid ship closely. I plotted her course in my *Atlas of Canada* with a ruler and a blue ballpoint pen: through the St. Lawrence Seaway; across Lake Ontario; then up through the seven locks of the Welland Canal, which traveled from St. Catherines to Port Colborne, raising the ship to Lake Erie, 570 feet above sea level. From Lake Erie the yacht would travel past the Pelee Passage, through the Amherstburg Channel and into the Detroit River. The *Britannia* would dock in Windsor at Dieppe Gardens. Tens of thousands, perhaps even a hundred thousand people, were expected to greet her.

Berenice and the Cantor postponed their move to their summer cottage near Belle River until after Dominion Day and the Queen's visit, so we could see the *Britannia*. Berenice and I planned how we might stay up almost the whole night before so we could get to Dieppe Gardens before sunrise, before the late-morning arrival of the yacht.

"I do not like large and noisy crowds," the Cantor said, and told us he would be happy just to look at any pictures that appeared in the newspapers or that we took.

"Don't worry, I'll have my Brownie ready," Berenice said.

And then the most astonishing news followed. My father received an invitation, along with several other city clergymen and community leaders, to meet the Queen and the Prince at Jackson Park, at a reception for the city's dignitaries. The wives of the clergy were also invited to this reception, which would be held near the sunken rose gardens. My mother could not leave her confinement. "I'm very disappointed I can't go," she said. But I could tell that her concern for the baby was so consuming that it did not matter to her at all.

"Maybe I can go as your wife, Rabbi," Berenice said to my father. The Cantor then sang out in falsetto, imitating Berenice's gestures, "Maybe I can go! Please! Take me! Take me!" And everybody laughed.

I will give the Queen your regards," my father promised my mother as he left the house in formal gray striped pants and a black jacket. Jackson Park was only a few blocks from our house, and my father left on foot in the warm July sun, his invitation in hand. Berenice and I accompanied him to the entrance of the park, which was guarded by the Mounted Police and where a crowd was gathering. We waved, and he waved back at us as he disappeared through the tall wrought-iron gates.

When my father came back from the reception he reported on his audience and conversation with the Queen. The Cantor and Berenice had waited at our house until he returned and described to us in extensive detail the setting near the sunken gardens; the local dignitaries and clergy standing in a long ceremonial queue, waiting their turn to speak to the royal couple; the young Queen's pastel-pink summer dress and her white shoes; the beautiful nosegay of orange and red roses, blue delphiniums, and yellow carnations that was presented by the four-year-old daughter of the mayor and which the Queen held the entire time in her gloved hands; the uniformed guard who stood behind her—"exactly like a statue, never once wavering"—holding a lavender parasol above the Queen's head to protect her from the hot sun.

"You know," my father told us, "Her Majesty has the most beautiful complexion I've ever seen. She is a great lady."

Berenice held her hand to her chest while my father spoke. She barely blinked. She was almost breathless.

When he was finally announced, my father approached the Queen. He bowed slightly from the waist.

"My wife is sorry she could not meet Your Majesty, but she is in confinement for our second child. Thank God, we already have a beautiful son."

The Queen was, as the song goes, a gracious queen, and said to my father, "We wish your wife good health and a very healthy baby."

"Thank you, Ma'am," my father said.

Then, my father told us, he was about to move on and leave the podium, thinking his moment with the Queen was over. Her Majesty stopped him. Her question was sweet and kindly.

"Rabbi, have you chosen a name for your new baby?"

My father held my mother's hand and smiled at her, then at all of us in the room. He paused and repeated his answer to the Queen.

"Berenice if it's a girl, Bernhard if it's a boy."

The Queen said, "Why, they are both lovely names."

Berenice suddenly started crying loudly, her bosom heaving up and down uncontrollably. "Oh, God. Oh, God . . . Rabbi . . . Bless you."

Finally the Cantor, his own eyes moist, gently led his wife, my mother's dearest friend, out of the bedroom and took her home.

My father seemed bewildered by the reaction he had caused. He started scratching his head. "I didn't mean to upset her. I know it's not the custom to name a baby after the living. I thought we'd make an exception."

My mother looked at my father, for she too had begun weeping, and for the first time in my life I heard her say to him, her voice choking, "I . . . love you. . . . You're a wonderful man."

Belle River

I spent the summer of my mother's confinement with the Cantor and Berenice at the lake. This was the same Lake St. Clair that Grosse Pointe and the Ford estate overlooked. Long ago I had gotten over the notion that Hannalore was rich and we were poor.

I always enjoyed our summer visits to the lake. Normally my parents rented a cottage next to the Cantor's, and we would spend the season as we did the remainder of the year, in close proximity. The summer I spent with the Cantor and Berenice was a season of great expectation and creativity, which made me forget the disappointment I had earlier felt.

My mother was going to have a baby. My father was at home, working hard on his book, "making tremendous progress," he said; he had received some crucial information from a colleague in Stockholm on the destruction of Nehardea. And the Cantor had begun working on his oratorio, a suite for six voices and piano called *L'olam Vo'ed*— "Forevermore." When the Cantor explained this to me he said it was "for all the *korbanot*," those who were sacrificed and died. "It will be sad but hopeful too, like all art should be, with the possibility of redemption."

The Cantor intended to find passages from the Psalms and weave them together, setting them to music. Each of the six voices would have its own theme, he told me, and each voice would visit the others and speak to them consolingly so no one would ever feel left alone. "The worst pain, Alexander, is the pain of being forever alone."

He walked all day with a Bible in hand, around the cottage lawn and along the shore. He hummed his new melodies and then went into the cottage to score them at the spinet, which he had brought with him from Windsor. In the evenings, Berenice would sit at the piano and play out the music the Cantor had written during the day, while he accompanied her by voice. Although she was a large woman, her hands were narrow and delicate, with long, thin fingers.

This collaboration was something new between them. I

had never heard Berenice accompany her husband at the piano. It cheered me up to listen to them, especially if I was beginning to feel lonely. Early one evening, while we walked along the beach, Berenice explained: "We have reached a new stage in our marriage, and I am more a part of things. Perhaps it's because he has taken on such an enormous task, the oratorio, and needs my help. I can't explain, but it makes me very happy, Alexander."

Berenice and I stopped and watched the horizon, where the sun had begun setting over the lake. There was no haze or clouds. When the sun slipped under the water, we saw a brilliant green flare as the vanishing light refracted through the atmosphere. Berenice let out a gasp of pleasure. "My God, I've heard about the 'green flash' all my life, but I'd never seen it! It's one of the most beautiful things I've ever seen! I have never seen such a perfect color or light. Like an emerald. It makes you want to follow it." She hugged my shoulder, bent over, and looked me in the eyes. Her breath smelled of peppermint. "You did see it, Alexander? Didn't you? Wasn't it beautiful?"

"Yes, Berenice. It was very beautiful."

*I*n the mornings, the Cantor made the rounds of his trees, which stood on the tiled area on the rise before the beach. Along either side, at the lakefront, were large old willow trees. The foreign cultivated palms stood apart, upright and dignified in their pots, amongst the sprawling and luxurious natives.

That year, the lake had begun to recede, part of a cycle of recession and replenishment that occurred over decades. One morning a sandbar arose and extended our beach. "See, Alexander," Berenice said. "The lake is a living, breathing thing. She is showing a bit of ankle." When we wanted to swim we had to cross the new sandbar and then wade farther out than usual into the lake.

Berenice was afraid I would be bored, and so she planned several outings. One day we might start out early and drive past Stony Point and then by Wallaceburg along the Canadian side of the St. Clair River to Lake Huron.

"Lake Huron is a great inland sea," Berenice explained to me as she pointed out its vastness, how we could not see across it although it was a particularly clear and sunny day. "A long time ago dinosaurs probably lived here and are buried under the lake. When you think of such a very long, long time ago, when other creatures roamed the earth, creatures that will never see the light of day again, it makes you realize how unimportant your own problems are. Anyway, when I think of dinosaurs, I consider myself absolutely tiny. And if I had been a dinosaur, I do not know where on earth I would have bought my shoes!"

Another day Berenice had an exciting idea. We would follow from shore part of the route of the *Britannia*. We would drive along the Canadian coast of Lake Erie and then turn up north along the Welland Canal to St. Catherines. "The Welland Canal is one of the great engineering wonders of the world, and it's right near us. We really should see it."

We set out in the morning. The Cantor woke early to prepare us deviled eggs and a salad platter with smoked perch. Berenice put them and several bottles of soft drinks in a cooler that went into the backseat of the car. It was another hot and sunny day. There were no clouds in the sky.

"It's almost tropical when you think about it. It's so green here, my eyes hurt!" She put on her old butterfly sunglasses. Two or three of the original rhinestones were missing. "Everyone thinks that Canada is so cold, but every summer the tropics come to visit us. Once upon a time, when the earth was tilted in a different way, Canada was a different place, it wasn't even Canada. It *was* tropical."

Opposite the shore of Lake Erie we passed endless fields of corn and wheat. Several miles before Wallacetown, we took an inland shortcut on our route to Port Colborne. We passed a sign to St. Thomas.

Berenice became excited: "Isn't this crazy and fun? When I was a little girl we used to take the *Père Marquette* to St. Thomas and change trains for Port Stanley. It was a popular lake resort. I loved that train ride. My brother and I had so much fun. Maybe we should take a trip to Port Stanley—"

"My uncle died in St. Thomas," I interrupted.

"Yes, I know," she said quietly.

"He was criminally insane, you know, and tortured dogs. He gouged out their eyes and cut off their private parts." I said this though I did not know if it was true. I said it calmly, as if I were indifferent to the horrifying facts. My parents never spoke anymore of my uncle Avner, and I had always been afraid to ask.

"Oh, no, goodness no!" Berenice told me. "Your uncle Avner wasn't a criminal or insane or mean or anything, though I never met him." She began speaking rapidly. "Even I didn't know your mother had a brother. I always told her about my older brother Teddy, who volunteered for the Haganah and moved to the Galilee. But she never mentioned she even had a brother except once, just after he died. She doesn't like to talk about it. Your father told me some of the details too.

"Avner was her older brother. At first he was a normal and intelligent child. Your mother and Avner walked to school together. He was a good boy and always looked after his little sister. Then he got a terrible disease. He started acting strange. I'm not sure how, exactly. They thought it was an emotional problem. Finally he just couldn't see or hear right anymore. He stopped speaking and couldn't walk. He couldn't control his bodily functions—you know what I mean. It was some kind of nerve disease. I sometimes wonder about doctors. They can be so cruel. They did try to help him, but they couldn't. They never can, not when it's really serious. That's why your grandparents put him away. They thought he would die quickly, but he lived many, many years after that."

Berenice stopped speaking for a few moments. The air blowing through the car windows was hot and humid. A large bumblebee buzzed across the windshield, then vanished out Berenice's window. She started talking again.

"I know it broke everyone's heart. I know that. Please don't tell your parents I told you this. They'd be angry at me, especially your mother. But you know, Alexander, I also think it's wrong to put someone away that you love. Even when they're terribly sick and you cannot bear to watch them suffer. It's like judging. It's like they are being punished twice, even though it's not their fault. Lots of things happen to people that aren't their fault. And your father's parents were worse, forgive me for saying so. They wanted to stop your parents' wedding. They thought your mother had bad genes. When they saw they couldn't change your father's mind, they moved back to Frankfurt. Everyone thinks your dear father is a pushover, but when it really matters he is one of the strongest men I know. Just think, if your father had listened to his parents, you wouldn't have been born!"

For a moment I saw the luminous letters of my name fading in the endless darkness of space. Their light pulled back into themselves, and they died like embers.

Suddenly Berenice slowed the car. I saw how her long foot in its pink sandal lifted off the accelerator and pressed gently on the brake. Her words slowed down too, became careful, measured. "Just think, soon your mother will have a new baby. God is blessing her. God blesses people who do things out of love, only we don't know what the blessing might be. I always wanted a baby too, you know, but the Cantor can't have one. They did a terrible operation on him, so we can't have children. I would have died if they did something as painful as that to me. I'm not that strong. When we first got married the Cantor would wake up at night, screaming. I knew all about it before we married, he never hid anything from me, but it didn't seem important to me then. I was in love and he loved me. He still tells me, 'Berenice, Berenice, thank you for not letting me live my life all alone.'"

Berenice pulled over to the side of the road and stopped the car. She was out of breath, panting. "Alexander, please get me a Coke from the cooler. I'm so thirsty. Take one for yourself, otherwise you'll get dehydrated too." She drank the whole bottle at once. After delicately wiping her wet lips with the corner of a lace handkerchief, Berenice took a photograph out of her purse. It was really half a photo-graph, cut down a previous center with an unsharp scissors. In the picture was a skeleton in striped rags with a dark, knotlike face. At first I did not realize who it was, but then

I knew it was the Cantor. He looked older in the picture than he was now, and this confused me.

"This was taken when he was liberated. He had almost starved to death." Berenice put the picture back into her purse. She smoothed back her hair, which was damp and glistening from the humidity and her perspiration. "The other half of the photograph was of Hannalore, but she cut herself out and destroyed it. I don't know who took the picture or how those two survived. They liked to collect twins to do experiments. They kept them in a barracks next to the compound for the Gypsies. 'Twins! Twins!' they called out whenever a new trainload of people arrived. Most of the twins were children and too young to survive. They did horrible experiments on them." Berenice was very nervous. Her voice wavered. "I shouldn't start telling you all this. I haven't even told your parents. I don't want to scare you or give you bad dreams."

"I'm not scared," I said.

"You mustn't tell either, please. Some things must always remain secret. Promise me."

"I promise."

After Berenice had told me everything, she seemed more relaxed. I had to sit on my hands, because they had begun to shake uncontrollably. Berenice did not seem to notice.

"Sometimes, Alexander, I think you are the only one I can really talk to. There are some things I could never tell your mother about, even though she is my dearest friend in the world.

"You're sensitive. If I had a son I would have wanted him to be just like you. Spending all this time with you makes me feel very close and blessed. I'm not always so happy on the inside as I seem on the outside. I envy the lucky girl who gets you when you get older. Anyway, just being with you makes me happy."

"Me too," I said, though as soon as these words escaped my lips I felt an awful regret, as if I had said something foolish or been made to agree to something I did not want. I did not want one day to make some girl lucky. What did that have to do with having a nice time with Berenice and going on our adventures? What she said made me uneasy. But it was also true, I thought. I did not lie when I said "Me too." I did love Berenice. She was my friend and treated me as she would an adult. But I had the unpleasant feeling that even loving words could be dangerous.

Once every other week I went with Berenice into Windsor to visit my mother. The intensity of my love for her did not diminish over the summer. Whenever we entered her room, she lay in bed, propped up on pillows.

"Berenice! Alexander! Thank you for driving all the way in this boiling heat to visit me."

It was a particularly hot summer, and the back of the house was without shade. The Great Goddess Asherah had died the year before. When the people from the city came to cut her down, my father read a eulogy from the Book of Proverbs, his voice rising above the sound of the chain saws: "'Strength and dignity are her clothing; and she laughs at the final day.'"

Most of the time, because of the heat, all the windows in my parents' bedroom would be open. One or two fans would be whirring, their faces turning this way and that, guardians of the atmosphere and the growing child in my mother's womb. My mother did not like air-conditioning. She thought it might make her sick. Bouquets had been placed in vases on the night tables and the large dresser. My father would pick fresh flowers from the backyard garden, mostly peonies, roses, and irises that my mother had planted in past years. Occasionally there were other visitors, women from my father's congregation, but when I came into the room with Berenice they got up from their seats, smiled, exchanged a few pleasantries, and quickly left. My mother always seemed relieved and happy to see us.

"Whew, I'm glad those *makhashefot* left," my mother would sometimes say. "Those witches are always trying to figure out if I'll—" She would stop herself and look at me for a moment. "Well, you know what I mean, Berenice. It gives me the creeps."

"Oh, they all love you, Sarah," Berenice would say. "They wish the best for you."

My mother rolled her eyes.

"Sarah, being cooped up every day is making you paranoid."

"Well, I guess I can't help that. I've always been a little paranoid."

"Ah, finally you admit it, Sarah!"

My mother would then change the subject and ask if I was having a nice time with Berenice.

"I've missed you both. What have you two been up to?"

I would begin to tell her about whatever outing we had gone on. Sometimes she would remain attentive and ask me questions. Other times, more so as the summer continued, she would lose interest as I tried to tell her some small detail of a particular outing, about the dinosaurs under Lake Huron, or the seven graded locks of the Welland Canal. "I think your mother's tired," Berenice would say. "The baby's sleepy and making your mother sleepy too." Then we would leave.

On our last visit of the summer, before we were about to go back to the lake, my mother told me I could put my hand on her belly.

"You can feel the baby kicking now, Alexander. Ooh.

Feel it? Gently, Alexander, not too hard now. Really, not too hard."

I felt the baby thump and kick, which filled me with such amazement that I yearned to stay there, pressing myself over my mother's stomach, feeling the baby moving about, swimming in its safe darkness.

Berenice tugged on my shoulder and insisted we go immediately.

"It's beginning to cloud over, Alexander, and I don't like driving in the rain."

I didn't want to leave. I couldn't help myself and burst into tears.

Berenice slowly pulled me off my mother and held me back tightly in her arms. "Come on, sweetheart. Come on." She rested her chin firmly on my hair. "Your mother's tired, Alexander, let's go. We'll be back soon. I promise."

I shook myself free of Berenice. I glared at her.

"My mother told me I could always stay home if I wanted."

"Go with Berenice, Alexander," my mother said, and closed her eyes.

Later, when we were driving back to Belle River, the sky turned dark purple. Berenice, who had been very quiet and thoughtful, now became excited.

"Oh, I love a real summer storm! With thunder and lightning! Nature in her fury and glory!"

Berenice turned on the radio. There was a tornado warning for the entire county.

"Just like in *The Wizard of Oz!*" Berenice said. "Now we really better hurry back and batten down the hatches."

We sped along the roadway. When we arrived at the cottage, the lake was choppy. The sandbar had disappeared under rolling whitecaps. Dark clouds rushed through the sky. "Wow!" Berenice said. The Cantor came out and said something about the palm trees. Berenice told him not to worry, they were used to tropical weather, but we would all try to help him bring them, one by one, closer to the house.

Suddenly it was too late. In the distance a great funnel began swirling and spinning over the lake.

A tornado was heading to shore.

Rain started falling in great wet sheets, and strong gusts blew sand in our faces. I had never seen a storm like this, but I was not afraid. I was a survivor who had held the door to his mother's womb shut for nine months, swimming in a dark and watery closet. I was smart and strong even before I was born. I wanted to stay outdoors and watch.

The Cantor was frantic. The beloved palms were trembling in their pots; they shook and bowed their leafy crowns. They begged for their lives. In the tremendous noise of the wind I thought I heard them cry out, "Save us! Save us!" But I wasn't moved to save them. I didn't care. I despised their weakness, their delicacy. If I had been them I would have been strong. I would fight! I thought the willows, with their great roots solidly in the earth, must be laughing at them. "Ha! You paragons of beauty! Now you're going to get it!"

The Cantor desperately tried to push all the palms closer together and tie the trunks with a rope, but the wind was too strong. Berenice tried to reassure him. "They're used to this kind of weather: it's tropical; they'll be okay. They'll bounce right back, you'll see." She began begging him. "Bernhard, let's go inside before it's too late." With all her strength, she pulled her frantic husband toward the house, and then realized I was standing there on the edge of the lake, resisting the wind. For the only time in my life she screamed at me. "Alexander! Are you crazy? Get into the cottage this instant! What has gotten into you today?"

There was a small half-cellar under the cottage, and we all three lay cramped in it as the wind whistled around the house. We heard a great terrifying noise like gunshots. And then suddenly the noise stopped. The Cantor wanted to get up immediately, but Berenice said no, we should wait a few more minutes. "We might be under the eye of the tornado. It's always quiet under the eye of the tornado, like a hurricane." We waited another minute, and finally the Cantor could bear it no longer. We climbed up and went outside.

The tornado had skirted the shore. All the palms had toppled over and crashed to the ground. Their trunks were fractured, and I saw their whitish-yellow insides, all fibrous and oozy. Two of the trees had fallen over each other like sticks, so that they made a cross like the golden crucifix Hannalore wore. Some of the willows had lost branches but were otherwise spared. They appeared relaxed in the eerie calm.

Then, for the first time, I saw a man—a man who once looked like a skeleton with a knotlike face, a man whom evil people had operated upon without anesthetic so he could never have children, a man who wrote the most beautiful melody I ever heard—I saw this man cry.

Several hours after the storm, we still had no telephone or electricity. The lake, in the brightening slice of late afternoon, was swollen and purple, like a bruise. A few shutters had been blown off the cottage, but otherwise surprisingly little damage had been done to it. A narrow serpent of sand had been carried by the tornado onto the lawn between the cottage and the lake.

Sometimes, my father had once explained in a sermon, God hides His face from His people, and it is at such times that disasters multiply.

Someone drove up the cottage driveway. It was Dr. Desjarlais's son, Mickey, who was sixteen or so and had recently learned to drive. He wore shorts and a thin, rain-soaked tee shirt that said "Walkerville Collegiate." At first I hardly listened to what he was saying, because I was staring, hypnotized, at the thick black hair that fell to his broad shoulders, his brown eyes, and at his strong hands as he gestured and spoke quickly. He was already a man. His father had sent him to bring us an urgent message. Finally I realized what he was saying. My mother had begun to lose the baby and had been taken to the hospital.

"My father said to tell you all not to worry," Mickey said, looking at the Cantor and Berenice. He did not seem to see me. "The Rabbi's wife will be all right, for sure."

I stood a long while and watched Mickey's back and calves as he walked and settled himself into his car. I longed to go with him and see my mother. It was a terrible longing, which I had never felt before. After Mickey drove down the gravel driveway and swerved onto the main road, I turned around and looked at the ground. My eyes were stinging. And I knew I was crying, not because my mother was losing the baby, but because Mickey had gone and I felt so alone.

I looked up. Berenice and the Cantor had left me where I was standing and were walking slowly toward the cottage. Berenice's arms were around her husband, supporting him. I watched them, saying to myself the whole time, "No. I am not afraid. I am not ashamed. Why should I be? Why should I be?" This finally made me feel better.

I felt almost proud.

I knew I was smart and strong even before I was born, and had a stubborn heart. I knew I could live my life all alone if I had to, and it would never even matter.

S h e b a

At the beginning of autumn, a few weeks after my mother lost the baby, Marla Cook and her mother came to our synagogue to hear the Cantor sing. It was Rosh Hashanah. As always, they sat in the back row. Marla had on a bright-red silk dress and the same extravagant necklace she had worn when I saw her on Tecumseh Road. Her mother was dressed in her usual black. Marla kept tugging on her mother's sleeve, pulling her back into her seat whenever she tried to get up and leave. Her mother finally gave in, and they remained seated until the end of the service.

When I was walking home, ahead of my parents, the Cantor, and Berenice, I heard a familiar nasal voice.

"I survived Texas, Mrs. Lot." Marla managed to be standing suddenly in front of me. "But I could still die at any time. The doctor told my mother my heart could shut off at any time. Like a stopwatch. Or I could simply blow a gasket."

"Where's your mother?" I asked.

Marla looked at me carefully, first with one eye, then with the other. Though I had seen her several times over the years, and once up close on Tecumseh Road, I suddenly realized that her eyes were farther apart than was normal, almost at the edges of her face.

"Am I my mother's keeper? My mother thinks if she takes me to visit all the different gods, maybe I'll live. She believes in appeasement. Like that filthy Chamberlain. He was her distant cousin. He's long dead now but a shame to the entire family. Anyway, I sent her home. I can walk much further myself now." She fondled her golden necklace that was studded with red and green jewels. They glittered in the afternoon sun. "They're all real," she said. "Emeralds and rubies, with a few diamond baguettes thrown in for luck. Very expensive. It once belonged to some duchess or empress, I don't remember. She had to give them up. She might have been killed if she'd kept them. Hard times call for hard choices, you know."

Berenice and my mother came over to us. Berenice said, "Hello, Alexander. Hello, young lady. I've seen you before. My name's Berenice. This is Sarah. What's your name?"

"The Queen of Sheba."

My mother gave Berenice a funny look, but Berenice kept talking as if nothing unusual had been said.

"Well, does the Queen of Sheba want to join us for lunch? We're all eating at my house."

"I might as well," Marla answered. "I might die this year. Unless your God wrote me in His 'Book of Life,' like the Rabbi said. But first I want to meet Eva Moore and Bijou, the Prince of Puppies. My mother won't let me have a dog, because if I die she'll have to take care of it."

By now Berenice and my mother were speechless.

A taxi drove up alongside us, and a woman got out. It was Marla's mother. She was a tall, elegant woman. She wore a strand of pearls over the collar of her black dress. She was clearly upset but was trying to control herself and appear calm and dignified.

"Marla, I've been looking all over for you. You know the car was waiting to pick us up. Why did you run off like that?"

"I was invited to lunch."

Mrs. Cook looked puzzled.

Berenice said to Marla, "You shouldn't have scared your mother like that." Then she said to Marla's mother, "I'm sorry. I didn't know you were looking for her, so I invited her. Would you like to join us?"

"No, no, I couldn't impose." She turned to her daughter,

her voice soft and imploring. "Let's go now, Marla, we really—"

"I'm going with *them*," Marla said firmly. "I was properly invited."

Mrs. Cook hesitated.

Berenice said, "It's all right. She can come. She's welcome."

Marla glared at her mother.

"Well, only if you remember to be a lady and say thank you. Please call a taxi when you're ready to come home. It's too far for you to walk. So don't try it. You have to promise. And promise not to chatter too much at these nice people. And be respectful of their customs."

Marla smiled very sweetly and promised.

As soon as we arrived on our block, Hannalore drove up in her convertible. Berenice and the Cantor tried introducing her to Marla.

Hannalore hardly seemed to be paying attention or even to see the strange young girl. She was all agitated, lighting cigarette after cigarette and throwing them on the ground without even smoking them. Marla said, "If you play with matches you're liable to get burned!"

Hannalore gave her a funny look, then continued to ignore her.

"*Die Italienerin*, she spoke against me in front of all the other servants." Hannalore's eyes kept blinking. "She knew today was my day off. She knew. I told her! 'Why today, Hannalore? Why today?' she kept saying. 'Why today? Is it a special *day*? Is it perhaps your *birthday*? You know we are having important guests! I need you *here*!'"

"It sounds like a misunderstanding to me," Berenice said. "You shouldn't be so upset."

"Oh, no! It is no misunderstanding! *Mon Dieu!* I can't stay there anymore. I went to Mademoiselle Dee Dee immediately this morning. She said I must move to find better *baxt*. I don't know what I'll do for another job. I'll starve!"

Marla said, "Here, take this if you need money. It's worth a small fortune." She took off her necklace and held it outstretched in her skinny hand. She turned it this way and that, so that it sparkled and flashed red and green constellations on the white siding of the Cantor and Berenice's house.

Hannalore ignored her and went on complaining about her Mrs. Ford. *"Die Italienerin hat mich beschimpft!"*

Marla repeated, this time shouting in her high nasal voice: "I said take this! It's worth a fortune! You can retire on it, you stupid woman, or whatever weird creature you are!"

Everyone was dumbfounded. Berenice and my mother, the Cantor and my father, all stood on the sidewalk in front of our two neighboring houses.

Hannalore finally turned to Marla, who was holding out the necklace.

"What? . . . I cannot accept such . . . such *bijoux* from a stranger. Do your parents know what you are doing?"

Marla became enraged.

"My parents? My parents? My mother gives me anything I want. I'm deformed. Can't you see? And I'm *dying!* Do you know what that's like? Do you?"

I saw Hannalore nod, but Marla didn't seem to notice. I held my hands tightly behind my back so they wouldn't shake.

Marla turned one eye, then the other, to our little group. "I'm an orphan too; my father is dead. Why wouldn't my mother let me have these things! I can do whatever I want with them."

Marla threw the necklace on the lawn.

Hannalore went over and picked it up. She held it to the sun and looked at it carefully. She began to cry. She turned to Marla in wonder. "Where did you get . . . such a beautiful thing?"

"I hate answering questions over and over. Don't you? A simple 'thank you' would do."

"Yes. Thank you. Thank you."

It suddenly occurred to me that Marla's giving and Hannalore's receiving united them in some way, but I did not know how.

Marla abruptly changed the subject and began talking very softly and sweetly to Berenice and my mother about Eva Moore.

"I think she's the most beautiful woman in the world. She just bought a marquise-cut emerald in my mother's store. I saw her myself, looking at it under the loupe. She knows her gems like a connoisseur. My mother said it was a perfect stone. I asked Miss Moore where Bijou, the Prince of Puppies, was. She said he was at home, watching television. Eva Moore said she wished people would leave poor Bijou alone. She really can't go anywhere with him in public anymore without people wanting his pawprint autograph. I said I could understand exactly how she felt." Marla began walking around all of us, her red silk dress fluttering about her, looking with one eye and then the other while she spoke. Slowly she managed to herd everyone into a small circle. "I wish I had a dog, but my mother won't let me have one. She's afraid I might die and then she'll have to take care of it. I told her if I died she could have it cremated and buried with me, like they do in some countries to the wives and servants." Marla looked directly at Hannalore. "Or my mother could spare its life and give the dog away. Plenty of people would be willing to take care of it, I'm sure. I don't believe it has to come with me that instant to heaven. . . ."

Marla was now becoming out of breath.

"You know, I'm really not hungry just now. . . . I think I'm ready to go home now. . . . I'm quite tired. Mrs. Berenice, would you call me a taxi? Call Checker; we have our account with them."

Berenice obediently went inside to make the phone call.

The rest of us waited silently outdoors for almost ten minutes until the taxi drove up. It was as if everyone had fallen into a trance.

When the cab arrived Marla walked over to me and said, "So long, Mrs. Lot." Ignoring everyone else, she turned away and climbed into the car. She did not wave or look back.

After Marla was driven away we went into the house. Berenice said she was going back to the kitchen to call Mrs. Cook. A few minutes later, when she returned to the living room, she made us all sit down. She stood in the middle of the room and explained how she had told Marla's mother about the necklace.

"I offered to bring it back to the store after Rosh Hashanah was over. 'Tell me a good time to come,' I said, 'so Marla won't find out.'" Here Berenice became teary-eyed. "But Mrs. Cook said to me, 'No, Mrs. Seidengarn, you mustn't bring it back. Never. Please. Do you understand? If Marla gave it away, then your sister-in-law must keep it. It belongs to Marla to do with as she pleases. She won't want it back. I'm so glad Marla's done a good deed by her own free will. I know she's a strange child, but she can be very wonderful and generous. Maybe your God will have mercy on her if you pray for her. God favors your people.'

"I told her that God was everyone's God and He didn't

play favorites. But Mrs. Cook said, 'Yes, of course He does, Mrs. Seidengarn. Just look around you.'"

"'But I have,' I told her. 'I have.'"

But Mrs. Cook remained adamant. "I know your people have suffered so much and are scattered, Mrs. Seidengarn, but they always bounce back and make themselves at home wherever they are."

When Berenice finished retelling her conversation, she remained standing a moment or two in the middle of the living room.

My mother was staring oddly, her hands holding her stomach. She did not seem to be in pain. I know now this gesture had become merely a reflex for her, for she had lost the baby only a few weeks before.

Hannalore was sitting in a corner, fingering the necklace, her mouth slightly open. Then she spoke. "No one ever gave me such a beautiful thing. Nobody ever did such a wonderful thing for Hannalore, nobody."

She blushed and looked up at her brother. "Of course, except Bernhard. Bernhard *hat mich gerettet*. Bernhard saved me."

The Cantor came over and gently patted his sister on her thin shoulder.

She looked up at him. "Remember?"

I looked over to Berenice. She was busy wiping her eyes with a handkerchief.

"Hannalore, Hannalore," the Cantor said. "Let's not

think about it now." He took the necklace in his hand. "Yes, Hannalore. It is really beautiful. The most beautiful present I've ever seen. I wish I could have given it to you."

Finally my father began quoting: "'Va'teetayn l'melech . . . And she gave the king a hundred and twenty talents of gold, and of spices very great store, and precious stones: there came no more such abundance as these which the Queen of Sheba gave to King Solomon. And so she turned and went to her own country, she and all her servants.'"

Key West

Several weeks after Marla gave her the necklace, Hannalore took a job in Key West, Florida. Her new employers, we learned, were not as rich or famous as the Fords, though they moved in the same circles and had once before asked Hannalore to work for them.

"And so it is a very happy ending. My *baxt* has improved," Hannalore told us when she came to say good-bye to her brother and sister-in-law. "And I will have a room that looks out on the sea! And you know, the island is almost shaped like a kiss! Well, perhaps not quite. For once it is a little lie I am making. But I will be living almost next door to the late Mr. Hummingway and his funny cats. They all have six toes!"

Berenice corrected her. "Hemingway, Hannalore, Hemingway."

Hannalore shrugged her shoulders. "It makes no never mind. I don't like to read in English." She paused and changed the subject. "And you know what? That *woman* asked me to stay. She begged me not to go. 'I will pay you more, Miss Hannalore! I will pay you more! What can I do to make you happy?' But I said like ice, 'Madame Cristina'—I used her first name—'I am sorry, but it is too late for such gestures.'"

Because of her new job Hannalore did not need to sell the necklace, but she had it appraised. She laughed, revealing her large crooked teeth. "*C'est vrai! C'est vrai!* It *is* worth a small fortune. It will be part of poor Hannalore's pension!"

For several weeks after Hannalore's departure, Berenice became preoccupied with Marla. She told me she had dreams about her. "I see her walking down a sidewalk or on the beach in the funny way she walks, and she jabbers away, and I can never remember what she has said when I wake up. She breaks my heart. What a strange creature she is. Like a totally different species."

My mother, on the other hand, never spoke of Marla and told Berenice that she didn't like to think about her.

One day Berenice finally had an idea. She would write to Eva Moore and invite her to tea with Marla.

She showed me the letter before she sent it:

Dear Miss Moore,

There is a very sick child who is one of your greatest ad-
mirers and I know would treasure spending even a little time
with you. Would you kindly accept an invitation to afternoon
tea at my house so you can meet her? The child's name is
Marla Cook. She says she met you once in her mother's jewelry
store.

Sincerely,
Mrs. Berenice Seidengarn

Eva Moore called Berenice the following week and
promised to come to tea, though she mentioned that she
did not recall ever meeting Marla or shopping in Mrs.
Cook's jewelry store. She told Berenice: "If you ever watch
me on television, Mrs. Seidengarn, you'll notice I'm not the
type of woman who spends much time in jewelry stores,
though I do humbly confess a weakness for clothes, which
I often make myself. The only ornaments I wear are the
pearls my mother gave me when I was a young woman.
Well, I look forward to our afternoon at four."

Berenice asked my mother and me to join them. "It will
be more festive that way. And it might keep Marla from getting overly excited."

The day of the big event, the Cantor spent several hours
preparing rich pastries and finger sandwiches. Berenice

polished her silver tea server and tray. She set the dining room table with a linen tablecloth and the hand-painted porcelain teacups she collected and displayed in her china cabinet.

Marla arrived by taxi at three, an hour early for tea. She wore the same red silk dress she'd had on when she came to synagogue a few weeks before. A diamond and sapphire brooch was pinned to her bodice, and several slender silver bracelets hung on either wrist.

"Is she here yet? Is Eva Moore really coming? I thought I might be late or she would leave early. I hope she brings Bijou with her. It's really my dying wish. Eva Moore is the most glamorous woman in the world!"

Marla began circling around Berenice's dining room table, inspecting all the tea objects, touching everything lightly with her fingertips, mumbling words like "Wedgwood," "Aynsley," and "Royal Doulton." She went into the living room and began lifting knickknacks off the side tables and putting them back down again. She looked behind the sofa and chairs. She checked for dust on the coffee table by sweeping her forefinger across the surface. Finally Marla got on her hands and knees and sniffed the carpeting.

"You certainly are excited, Marla," Berenice said. "You don't want to wrinkle your pretty dress. Anyway, don't you worry, we'll have a lovely time. How is your mother?"

"I must tell you something, Mrs. Seidengarn, in all confidentiality," Marla said. "The woman you met is really not

my mother. She's my aunt. My mother was a Polish count-
ess, but she died when I was a baby, and my father abandoned me. Miss Eva Moore could adopt me if she wanted.
You might want to broach the subject; it would be too forward for me to do so. You might tell her I could take care of
Bijou. I could walk him and feed him. I'd be very useful to
have around. You must tell Miss Moore. You must. My
mother—I mean my aunt—will just have to give me up. I
only call her my mother to save her delicate feelings, since
she did try her utmost to raise me. She'll just have to do
what's best for me!"

My mother had been watching the whole time and said
to Berenice, "I'd like to go over the menu with you in the
kitchen, Berenice, okay?" A moment later Berenice returned
to the living room and whispered to me that my mother
wasn't feeling well and had gone home through the back
door.

Eva Moore did not show up to Berenice's tea.

At half past four the telephone rang. Later Berenice told
me what had happened. Miss Moore's personal secretary
had called. "I'm so sorry, but Miss Moore is indisposed. She
has a touch of laryngitis, and the terrible thing is that Barbara Stanwyck is in Detroit and will be coming specially to
Windsor to be interviewed for Miss Moore's show. I know
you will understand that a professional like Miss Moore
must preserve her voice for the interview. She sends her
regrets."

Berenice was trembling when she got off the phone. She was terrified of telling Marla what had happened, but as soon as Berenice hung up Marla said flatly, staring into space, "Eva Moore must die."

Marla then turned to Berenice and said cheerfully, "Oh, Mrs. Seidengarn. Yoo hoo! *Mrs.* Seidengarn! When you stop quivering, would you please kindly call me a Checker?"

Frankfurt am Main

My father's grandfather, who had traveled at the turn of the century with the exiled prince of Persia, had been a citizen of Frankfurt, a book dealer on the famous Untermainkai, and an amateur scholar. My great-grandfather was already an elderly, albeit still vigorous, man when he escaped to Canada with his daughter and son-in-law, my father's parents, and a trunkful of his most precious books.

My great-grandfather died before I was born, and I was given his name, Aryeh Alexander. I had been vaguely aware of this fact from earliest consciousness, even before my father told me how my very own existence was announced in the heavens.

I was aware that my name had been in use before and had once accompanied a different life than mine, a life that in my early childhood I could not really imagine, even from the picture of the very old man in a top hat that stood framed on the mantelpiece, a figure ancient and full of days, holding a small shy boy, my father, by the hand.

I did not really know what to make of all this, except that sometimes I might pretend I was really two people— not twins, because twins, I knew, did not have the same names, but rather two heavenly bodies orbiting each other, two souls locked up one within the other. Sometimes, when I thought things over to myself, debated and tried to analyze the small world that stood before my evolving consciousness, I found myself to be of differing, contradictory opinions, which I attributed then and attribute even now to this awareness of a borrowed and duplicated name.

My father's parents were both university professors and had become rigorous and unyielding freethinkers. They had grown up in Frankfurt, in different neighborhoods, and had gone to Heidelberg, where they met as students. After their studies they both received academic appointments there, my grandfather in the Department of German Literature and my grandmother as one of the first women to teach in the Department of Physics.

My father was born in 1933, the year they arrived in Toronto.

My grandparents had, from what my father later told me, been opposed to his change from a university career to the rabbinate. Though he himself never put it in such harsh terms, they never forgave him. They were intolerant and considered all religion, especially the idea of a "revealed in His creation" personal God, as a betrayal, a physical abomination. My father had always pardoned them and sought to explain their behavior. "They cannot accept what they cannot see with their own eyes. But it is not only our eyes that see, Aryeh Alexander."

When my father was born, his parents were already in their mid-forties.

"Have children when you're young, Alexander," he told me. "When you're young enough to change and learn from them. My parents were too old and had been through too much. They were off schedule. I suppose they never even expected me to come along after all those years. I never have apologized for the shock I must have caused them, though not to do so may seem contrary to the commandment 'Honor your father and mother,' but I couldn't apologize for that! Otherwise I wouldn't be here! Nor would you!"

My great-grandfather, that author of *Auf den Spuren Abrahams entlang des Euphrat*, the man who left his own young family for three years to follow a defunct Persian prince through Mesopotamia, took the unexpected child of his own child's middle age under his wing and raised him.

"I always pretended my Opa was younger than my parents," my father once told me. "He was vigorous and optimistic. A sage and a nanny rolled into one. My parents were content to place me in his daily care and to save on the expense of a governess. They did not want to concern themselves about a small being so seemingly remote from their own intellectual pursuits. And perhaps they were pleased to keep the old man occupied."

Shortly before I was born my grandparents moved back to Frankfurt. It had never stopped being their home. We never saw my grandparents after that. They did not come to Canada to visit, and we did not go to Germany.

They still loved Frankfurt and found forgiveness for it in their hearts. All their frustrations and rage had been turned against an unseeable and unknowable God, but the calm waters of the Main, the rebuilt neighborhoods of Sachsenhausen on its southern banks, and the people who lived there were as precious to them as before.

My only contact with my grandparents was my yearly birthday greeting. I would receive a printed card, unsuitable for a child, which used the formal, the distant "you"-in-your-separate-and-faraway-world construction—*Herzliche Grüsse zu Ihrem Geburtstag*—and a modest check drawn on a Swiss account. The heavy paper of those green-lined checks was always covered with my grandmother's tall, spiky, top-heavy handwriting, somehow reminding me of the bulrushes that hid baby Moses. Over the years there was an unbending observance of the never-changing sum, and the more serene swaying of my grandmother's signature at the bottom.

All the time I was growing up my father would contemplate visiting his parents. He would write them and say he would like to visit, but they always rejected him. "We will be traveling the entire summer in Italy," they would respond, their usual "in the footsteps of Goethe" itinerary, or they might answer: "Our friends from Heidelberg will be staying with us that month, and our house is so small." My father never showed his disappointment. "Oh, it's good they're so busy. I hope I will have so many things to do when I'm their age."

W hen I was fourteen a telegram was delivered to our house. My mother answered the door and immediately went upstairs with the unopened envelope to my father's study.

I followed.

The telegram was from Frankfurt. My father opened the envelope and read that my grandfather was dying. The telegram simply and formally said: *"Ihr Vater ist todkrank."* My grandmother did not say whether my father should come or not. She did not indicate whether my grandfather wished to see his only child again before he left this world.

My father immediately announced he would go to Germany.

This decision enraged my mother.

My mother's face turned white except for the tip of her fine nose, which stayed strangely pink and despite the grave circumstances seemed clownlike and comical to me. She trembled but still managed to say everything she wanted to say, almost calmly, considering her anger. Clearly she had been waiting for years to say these words and knew that the day of opportunity had come. She spoke almost in a chant, as if she were reciting a psalm.

"They have shunned you and me for fifteen years.

"They have shunned the living.

"They have granted forgiveness on behalf of the dead."

She then said, slowly, sarcastically, *"Das haben sie vergeben! Nur das! Für die Toten. Den Mördern haben sie vergeben!* That they can forgive! Just that!" I was amazed, because I had never heard my mother speak German before. I had assumed she did not know any, except perhaps a few isolated words. She switched back to English. "They have no right to do that! But we will not get sidestepped into that issue. They are crazy. We all have to make compromises. They never did." Then she spoke slowly again, enunciating every word. *"Let them die on their own."*

"Sarah! They are my parents! I will not have you—"

My mother interrupted. "You just don't see! I'm sure they would prefer it. They didn't ask you to come! The telegram they sent is only a formality. They are very formal people. If you go, you will only remind them of their greatest disappointment. You!"

My father turned very pale. After a long pause he spoke slowly:

"They are my parents. They were partners with God in my creation, even if they were selfish and foolish. I have to go. I have no choice. If only for my own self." He looked away, staring out the birdcage to where the Goddess Asherah once stood. "I have to go, Sarah. If only for myself."

There were now tears in my mother's eyes, but her voice did not waver. "'If only for myself?' And what about *myself?* I've been punished enough. How many of *my* selves, my babies, died over the years? How many? Seven? And only that one I got to keep?" My mother suddenly pointed to me, and though I was far away at the entrance to the room, I felt as if I had received an electric shock. Until then I had imagined I was watching the scene from a great distance. My mother continued, her voice rising. "The rest I had to give back. Back to that same partner in your creation! My babies all died, your babies too, their grandchildren! Did they ever come see us? Did they ever once say, 'We are sorry you lost the baby'? Did you ever even tell them in your always forgiving letters? Did they ever care to know?"

Both my parents were now exhausted and said no more. My mother brushed passed me and hurried downstairs. Her words burned in my ears. "And only that one I got to keep?"

The next day my father traveled for the first time to Germany. He arrived several days before his father died.

One evening before my father returned, the doorbell rang. My mother received a telegram. She read the yellow sheet, then carefully tore it up. She walked into the downstairs bathroom and flushed the little pieces of paper down the toilet.

She came out and said calmly:

"Well, your father will be back tomorrow, two weeks to the day. He's flying into Detroit via New York."

The following morning, the day of my father's return from Frankfurt, my mother took a train to Toronto. I was at school. I had not even seen her pack—she must have done so after I'd left for my classes. The evening before, when she received the telegram, and that morning at breakfast, she behaved in the same reserved way she had during my father's entire absence. She had barely spoken even a sentence at a time to me, except when she received the telegram from Germany and announced that my father would return the following day.

When I got home from school, Berenice was waiting for me in the living room. Though my mother always kept the house meticulously clean, Berenice made a pretense of straightening up.

"Your mom went in a hurry to Toronto. She needed some time to herself. Don't you worry. I know my Sarah, and I'm sure she'll be back soon. She loves your father so much. She knows she can't help that. He is such a beautiful man. Anyway, your father will be home tonight from a very long trip, so let's try and make everything as comfortable and pleasant for him as possible. Do you want to go with me and Bernhard to the airport? I think it would be nice for your father to see you."

I said I would.

When my father arrived at the gate there was a tall old woman with him. She was thin and wore a finely tailored black skirt and a jacket over a frilly blue blouse. She moved very gracefully alongside him. She had white hair that was carefully coiffed. Her eyes were blue.

This was my grandmother. My father spotted us, and we all watched as he pointed us out to her. He was not smiling.

As they approached I heard her say to my father, *"Er sieht nicht krank aus."* My father answered her in English. I had never before heard him sound exasperated. "Please, Charlotte"—I was surprised that he called her by her first name, which he pronounced in the German way, where the name is subdued and broken into three syllables—"I have told you several times, Charlotte, Alexander understands several languages, and I have also told you as many times that he is not sick."

My grandmother turned her gaze away from him.

My grandmother was introduced to the Cantor and Berenice and extended her hand to them. It was a slender and finely wrinkled hand, with closely trimmed nails. The Cantor and Berenice seemed genuinely surprised when they realized who she was. It was clear that my mother had not told Berenice, as she had not told me, everything the telegram said. She had not told Berenice that her husband's mother was coming, the real reason for my mother's sudden departure to Toronto.

"*Es freut mich sehr,*" my grandmother said. "My son has told me about you both. You are such good friends to him."

She then gave her hand to me. "Aryeh Alexander. You are named after my own father. Are you like him?" She did not give me a chance to answer. "He was an adventurous man. Always a traveler. Quite careless. Always on the go, go, go.

"Your father says you are very smart and will finish high school two years early. I suppose that is possible in this lackadaisical country."

My father asked, "Where's Sarah?"

Berenice said, "She had to go to Toronto."

"Toronto!"

Berenice took him by his arm and led him slightly away

from our little group. "She just needs some time. She just needs a little time."

My grandmother raised her eyebrows.

The following day my father took the train to Toronto. While I was at school, Berenice took my grandmother on a little drive around Windsor. They then went through the tunnel to downtown Detroit. My grandmother bought some dark dresses and a pair of black orthopedic shoes.

That evening, while my father was still in Toronto, my grandmother and I went to Berenice's for dinner.

The Cantor asked my grandmother how she liked her trip to Detroit with Berenice.

"Your wife was very generous with her time. But I must say it is such an uncivilized place. I was actually frightened by the people, though, of course, I said nothing."

"Oh, Sarah and I love it there," Berenice said. "I thought you said you liked the stores and shopping."

"Where we come from," my grandmother said, looking gravely at Berenice, "my husband and I are treated with deference." She turned to the Cantor. "This dinner you have prepared is quite delicious. I see well that you are from the Elsass"—she used the German name Elsass instead of the French Alsace—"for it combines the elements of many exquisite cuisines."

The Cantor thanked her for her compliments. "Yes, Madame, the Alsace is famous for its cuisine. You will excuse me, but I need to lie down. I'm not feeling well." He then left the table.

My grandmother said, "We should be going back to your parents' house now, Alexander. It is next door, isn't it?" This was the first time she had addressed me since her arrival at the airport.

Before she went into the guest room for the night, my grandmother said, "It was not my idea to come here. It was his, and yet another mistake at that. I have my own life. I'm not a helpless old woman. And I want to go home."

She looked at me for a moment, as if trying to determine whether I understood.

"Home for me will always be where my husband and I grew up, where we first learned to speak, where our culture is. I hope you can understand that, Aryeh Alexander. And your home is here in this place with your father and mother. Tell me, are you happy?"

"Yes."

"Well, I am glad to hear that. *Gute Nacht*, Aryeh Alexander."

And she closed her door.

*T*he next day my father returned to Windsor. My mother did not accompany him, but he reassured me. "Mother will be back soon. Oma is returning to Germany tomorrow. She doesn't like it here that much anyway."

I did not witness any discussions between my father and his mother on these points. For the rest of her brief stay my grandmother remained in her room. My father brought her dinner on a tray. All he said to me while we ate our own dinner in the kitchen was: "Oma has a nice little house in Frankfurt, and friends, and a woman who comes to help her three times a week. She even has her own 'birdcage.'"

The following morning my father took his mother to the airport in Detroit.

"Good-bye, Aryeh Alexander," she said just before leaving our house. She kissed me lightly on either cheek. She did not look back when she walked out the front door.

My mother returned on the evening train from Toronto.

Houston

*F*or several years we did not see Marla or her mother. They no longer came to services on Rosh Hashanah, sitting in the back row and leaving before the end.

The evening after Eva Moore failed to show up for tea, Berenice had called Marla's mother. She apologized for raising Marla's hopes, only to have them dashed.

"I feel so awful. I was only trying to help, Mrs. Cook. I wanted to do something nice for Marla."

"Oh, it is not your fault at all, Mrs. Seidengarn," Mrs. Cook said. "Marla gets herself all excited about things and, of course, finds herself disappointed. Certainly it's not fair how she suffers. But what can anyone do? I do not know why God is always punishing her. She's done nothing wrong. And I have always tried to do the right thing, to make up for the past, but I see that I'm deluding myself."

"If there's anything I can do," Berenice said.

"From time to time when you think of her, pray to your God. Please ask Him to be less harsh. My Marla is an innocent."

As my father had told my grandmother, I was scheduled to graduate two years early from high school, which in Canada lasted through the thirteenth grade. In the early spring of grade thirteen I was approaching sixteen. I had already been accepted to the University of Toronto and to McGill University.

One day my father heard from Mrs. Cook. She was calling from Houston.

"I'm sorry to call you, Rabbi, but I have a favor to ask. Marla is here at the Texas Children's Hospital. She is not doing well. She keeps asking for your son. Would you let him come to see her? I will take care of the expenses, of course. Do you think he would mind? She has so few close friends."

"Marla Cook is very sick," my father said when I got home from school. "She would like to see you. You see how it is that we can affect others in ways we could never imagine. You must have been very nice to her, even in the brief times you spent together, for her to want to see you so badly."

A few days later my parents took me to the airport to catch a plane to Houston. My mother went over the tickets, explaining how to find the connecting flight in Chicago. "I'm proud you're willing to do this *mitzvah*, Alexander. You are stronger than I am. I could never face that unfortunate child again." Before I boarded the plane, my mother asked a stewardess to look after me on the flight.

Mrs. Cook was waiting for me at the gate in Houston when I arrived. She looked the same as on that Rosh Hashanah afternoon when I saw her up close, the day when Marla gave Hannalore the necklace.

"How was your flight?"

"Fine."

"Thank you for coming. Marla is so grateful you're here."

It was very hot outside, even though it was only March. The air was heavy and sweetly fragrant with flowering trees. A limousine waiting for us outside the terminal drove us straight to Texas Children's.

Marla was in a private room, lying in bed, propped up

on pillows. She had an oxygen mask on her face, which she asked her nurse to take off when I entered the room.

The nurse hesitated.

"I said take it off. Now! I'll manage without it for a while. Or shall I hold my breath like a child? Then if I die you'll be blamed and won't get paid."

During this entire outburst Marla's body barely moved, only her head and the features of her face. She had makeup on. Then with great effort she pulled off the light blanket that was covering her body. Marla was not wearing a hospital gown but was dressed as I had always seen her, as if she were going to a party or about to pose for a portrait. Her dress was blue velvet, with white satin bows on the puffed sleeves. On her forehead she wore a large blue gemstone set in silver. This beautiful jewel was pinned somewhat awkwardly to a narrow red headband.

"Hello, Mrs. Lot." Even from the stillness of her bed Marla seemed to be circling me, herding me in with her strange, far-apart eyes in the same way she had shepherded us together on the sidewalk in front of Berenice's house that Rosh Hashanah several years before.

"Hello, Marla. How are you?" I did not like being called Mrs. Lot, especially in front of strangers such as the nurse sitting at her bedside.

"Do you like my sapphire? It belonged to a defunct Estonian baroness of Russian descent, who fell on hard times. 'Oh, the troubles this jewel has seen!' It saved her life. She sold it and bought her way to Canada. She died, though, of heartbreak, the heartbreak of finding herself impoverished if nevertheless alive. An ingrate, if you ask me. She deserved to die. Do you covet this jewel?"

"No, why should I?"

"Well, you shouldn't. 'Thou shalt not covet.' I'd have given it to you for visiting me, but it's only appropriate for a debutante or an aristocratic woman. Are you a debutante or an aristocratic woman?"

Suddenly an entire group of doctors, nearly a dozen, came crowding into the room. They were led by an older physician.

"Here is King Solomon," Marla said to me.

She looked carefully at the senior doctor, focusing with one of her eyes. He was a handsome man with gray-blond hair. She raised one of her sticklike arms in a weak but sweeping gesture.

"'Happy are thy men, happy are these thy servants who stand continually before thee, and who hear thy wisdom.'"

The senior doctor smiled and answered with great dignity: "'And the Queen of Sheba came to Solomon to prove him with riddles. And Solomon answered her all her questions: there was nothing hid from the king, which he told her not.'"

Marla replied: "'Ah, but when the Queen of Sheba saw all of Solomon's wisdom, there was no more spirit in her.'"

Marla took in a deep breath before continuing:

"Well, Dr. Cooley, I'm on a steady decline, as you and your attending ministers well know. I suppose I'll be dead by next week. Am I right?"

The doctor seemed shaken; his eyes grew moist. He tried to regain his composure.

"Not if we can help it."

"But you cannot help it!"

Dr. Cooley then turned to me. "Ah, Sheba, is this the beau you have told me about? He's as good-looking as you said."

"No. *That* is Mrs. Lot, whom I once found transformed into a pillar of salt, but unlike me, he has luckily recuperated from such a bizarre affliction and moves about quite unrestricted."

I felt myself turning very red with everyone in the room now scrutinizing me. I looked down at the tiled floor so as not to see them.

I heard Mrs. Cook say: "Dr. Cooley, may I have a few minutes with you? Marla, Alexander, excuse us." When I raised my eyes I saw the doctor and his entourage leaving the room, following Mrs. Cook.

Marla looked at me with the eye opposite the one she had used to look at Dr. Cooley.

"They are discussing my funeral arrangements, no doubt. I hope you will attend. I have planned something quite touching. Could the Cantor sing something sweet and sad? Something High Holidayish?"

Later, when we were alone, standing in the hospital solarium, Mrs. Cook apologized.

"Marla says cruel things that she doesn't mean. She can't help herself. That's how she deals with her pitiful life. But I know she has found a friend in you. Most of us do not understand that we might see each other only a few brief times in a single lifetime and yet be eternal friends." Mrs. Cook gently rested her hand on my shoulder. "Marla is drawn to your soul, Alexander. Your people have the most dazzling and vivid souls. Since Marla has always been so very close to that other world where only souls exist, she is able to see and love yours."

Mrs. Cook asked me if we could sit for a moment. We faced each other from two vinyl-covered chairs. She looked around her. No one had entered the room.

"You know, Alexander, my late husband tried to save some of your people. He traveled in Europe on a forged Swiss passport, serving as a middleman, so to speak. He told me things didn't often work out as planned, the deals and barters and visas. I always believed him, but I don't know what to believe or do anymore. I don't really know what he did. My husband acquired many treasures from your people, and I suppose that is why your God is angry with us. But I don't understand why Marla should suffer.

Why Marla? She's an innocent. She knows nothing. She just makes things up. She wasn't even born then."

I returned to Windsor the following day. At the airport in Houston, Mrs. Cook said she would never forget how kind I had been to come and see her daughter. "I do not think she will live another week. She doesn't want me to bury her in the ground or have a tombstone. She says it would weigh her down. She wants to be cremated. Do you think that is right? It seems awful to me."

I said I did not know.

When I finished repeating this to my mother and Berenice on the ride home from the Detroit airport, the two women began to cry. I never told them about Mrs. Cook's late husband. Berenice, who was driving, pulled onto the shoulder of the highway to stop the car. My mother, who had always beheld Marla with aversion and fear, cried with the least control and restraint. To calm herself, she began to recite several Psalms that she knew from memory. She prayed out loud yet softly and in a cracking, mournful voice, the voice of something breaking. "'He makes the storm a calm, so that the waves thereof are still . . . and He brings them to their desired haven.'"

When we finally arrived back home, my father came to the door. During the time that my mother and Berenice had gone to pick me up at the airport, Mrs. Cook had called and told him that Marla had died.

We did not go to the early-morning mass that was held for Marla at the church in Walkerville, because even on such a sad occasion my father did not think it would be proper.

"They have their beliefs and we have ours," my father said. "I spoke to Mrs. Cook, and she understands." Then he said, in awe, in the same tone he had used years before when telling us about his meeting with the Queen, "Mrs. Cook is a great lady."

We joined up with Mrs. Cook and twenty or so mourners who came from the church service to the docks of the Windsor Yacht Club. From there we set sail in several small boats for Peche Island, a nature preserve that sat at the entrance of the Detroit River into Lake St. Clair. In the distance, Peche Island had begun to turn green from the early-spring weather. Mrs. Cook asked my parents, the Cantor, Berenice, and me to join her on her sailboat. It was a mild April day. The sun broke through the clouds overhead and began shining brightly. Small patches of mist rose from the surface of the water. Four or five boats carrying the other mourners followed us in a dignified procession. When we neared Peche Island, Mrs. Cook asked the pilot to drop the sails and let the boat drift. The other boats took up positions in a small crescent around us. Mrs. Cook, dressed in black, as I had always seen her, stood up from her bench and stretched her arms over the water. She held her hands high and in one gesture emptied the urn of her daughter's ashes. The ashes assembled themselves like a pillar of cloud over the water. A brilliant shaft of sunlight drove through the cloud, and for an instant it seemed on fire. The marvelous pillar stood still a moment, hesitated, then moved slowly away from our boat. "Don't look back," I said. And the pillar disappeared.

The Cantor rose to sing a melody he had composed for the occasion. It was as sweet and sad as Marla had wished. "I dreamed of it the night before," the Cantor told us later. But the melody seemed familiar to me, and I could not tell when or if I had really heard it before.

And when the Cantor rose and sang above the waters of the river, he sang in Hebrew and then in English so Marla's mother and her people would understand. His pure yet powerful voice floated above the surface, mixing with the vanishing patches of mist that still hovered there. His voice spread out, surrounding all the gently drifting vessels that accompanied Marla on this final journey:

> "V'atah lech l'kaytz, v'tanuakh. . . .
> And go thou on thy way: for thou shall rest,
> and stand up for thy reward at the end of days."

On our drive home from the yacht club, everyone was quiet. My father broke the silence.

"Alexander, you did the most wonderful kindness when you went to visit your friend. And this kindness, which forms the true substance of angels, will escort you and protect you, as all our good deeds do, every day of your life."

East of Ashshur

At times in the past I'd had vague thoughts of isolating myself, of withdrawing into myself. I suppose, looking back, that I had begun to do this even as a child, when I would often sit alone, playing silently by myself, contemplating the endless darkness of space and my luminous, celestial name.

I knew that at Creation, God performed *tzimtzum*. He withdrew into Himself, contracting His very being, and made within Himself an isolated place in which to set His universe—an infinite creation within an even greater infinity. There He organized all the attributes of His being in harmony, in the balance so naively depicted in my father's incunabulum of the Sefirotic Tree. This was something I then felt I needed to do for myself.

When I had thought before of my own need for isolation, I did not know how I would begin or how long I might be able to endure it or what it might accomplish for me. It was always a barely articulated thought. Sometimes I simply fantasized, as children so often do, of running away. But where? I think my walk to Tecumseh Road, the afternoon the children died, when I felt myself being controlled by outside forces, was an unconscious pursuit of this common childhood fantasy.

I had always figured I would know what to do when the time came, if it ever did. Sometimes I thought it would never happen, this contraction and isolation. Other times I thought I could endure an act of isolation forever. I knew there were holy men and ascetics who had lived apart and alone, far away in the wilderness, but this was not my purpose. I did not want to live alone in a wilderness. I did not want to be holy. I did not want to be closer to God or to be like Him. My father at first thought this must be my motivation, and my mother assumed that I was finally and simply going crazy.

The morning of my sixteenth birthday arrived after several weeks of warm weather. We had always celebrated my birthday according to the Hebrew calendar, and that year my birthday had wandered backward with the conjunctions of the moon from my Gregorian, solar-determined, July birth to the somewhat milder days of June.

Before lunch Berenice came over and asked if I would help the Cantor move the palm trees onto the backyard patio. Years earlier, after the tornado at the lake destroyed his beloved trees, Berenice bought him new trees, and he began cultivating them again. He had been so distraught that summer that he had wanted to sit shiva for his palms, but Berenice talked him out of it. "Trees are not people, Bernhard," I overheard her saying at the time. She spoke gently despite her imposing height. "It's not right, Bernhard. Trees are not people. And Sarah's just lost her baby. It just wouldn't be right."

Though he was now only in his early forties, the Cantor's health had begun to deteriorate quickly. He was less energetic than before. There was a great change in him even as compared to the time of Marla's funeral in March, when he sang on the sailboat drifting near Peche Island.

Dr. Desjarlais said he needed to take things easier. "We're all getting older, I suppose."

Though the Cantor continued for a while to sing in the synagogue, his voice lost its power and luster. He still tried to compose in his free time. The oratorio he had worked on during the summer of my mother's unfortunate confinement was long completed and lay in some drawer. It had never been performed. At first he had sent it to music publishers and to choral groups across the country, but it was always rejected, and he soon gave up trying.

"One day it will be discovered," Berenice told me. "One day it will, for sure. That's how these things happen. And then everyone says, 'Oh, of course, I know that piece. What a work of genius!'

"I keep telling the Cantor that. It meant so much to him and to me, since I helped him with it. For once I felt like his Muse. He even said so. He said, 'Berenice, you are my real Muse.'"

The morning of my birthday, the Cantor wanted to help me move the trees, but it was clear he did not have the strength to do so. Instead he showed me where to place them.

One by one I moved the palms out of the Palmenhaus, rolling them myself on their low-wheeled platforms. I had noticed that I was becoming strong, that my shoulders and chest were filling out. My legs were stronger too. I secretly hoped I might become as beautiful as Mickey. If only I were as beautiful as Mickey, I began thinking to myself, I would never have to feel alone.

I arranged the palms in a circle on the patio. Years before, when Berenice replaced them, she bought similar-size trees to the ones that were destroyed, so that their loss would be less obvious and painful. She had gone to great trouble and expense, ordering trees from Florida and California and even Cuba. In doing so she used up a small inheritance she had long saved from the sale of her parents' house in Outremont. Berenice told me: "It's a funny coincidence, but my brother used his share to help plant a date grove in the Galilee."

The new trees Berenice purchased after the tornado had flourished. Some would soon be too big for the greenhouse.

"I'm afraid you will have to send them to the Sorbonne, after all," I told the Cantor.

He laughed. "Soon you will have to go with them, Alexander, now that you have grown up so nicely and are graduating."

"But I don't speak French as well as they do."

"Berenice will teach you!"

At that moment Berenice walked out the kitchen door with my parents. She had made a surprise luncheon party for my birthday.

"Look," Berenice said. "We even have a special guest!"

Hannalore appeared at the doorway and followed everyone outside.

I had not seen Hannalore in several years, since she'd left the Ford household and moved to Key West, where Mademoiselle Dee Dee promised her better luck. We had all imagined that she led a life in the balmy shade of glamour on that island of artists and writers and the rich. But now, like her brother, Hannalore looked tired and pale. She had a mild tremor in her hands that I had never noticed before. Her head nodded continuously, as if she were quietly answering questions. She gave me a light hug, and kisses that fell on the air in front of one and then the other of my cheeks. I felt repelled by the stale warmth of her breath, but I stood politely. When I was little she had never hugged or kissed me.

"Well, our *rêveur* has certainly grown up. *Notre petit prince!*" Hannalore still wore her little golden cross over a starched white blouse. We all sat at the glass table in the middle of the patio, surrounded by the tropical trees.

"See, Hannalore, it's just like Florida!" Berenice said.

Hannalore smiled vaguely. "Too much sun, too much sky-blue ocean, can be a curse. When Bernhard and I were children we had the spring and summer, the fall and winter. I have missed the change of seasons."

After lunch the Cantor slowly went indoors and came back out with a chocolate and strawberry cake he had made. "Voilà, La Suprême de Hannalore! You will forgive me, Alexander, that I have named your birthday cake after my sister, but she is visiting from so far away. Still you must do the honors and blow out the candles."

After I did so, Hannalore became more animated. She

picked delicately at her serving of cake, though she hardly ate.

"Bernhard was always the best baker around! He could always do everything!"

"I wish I could bake as well as the Cantor," my mother said.

Then, because it was already an old joke among them, the Cantor and Hannalore added, "And speak French as well as Berenice!"

They all laughed. Even my mother and father, holding hands in a rare public show of affection, joined in the chorus when the Cantor and Hannalore said, "Berenice, Berenice, *redd wie d'r de schnawel gewachse isch!*—Just speak the way your beak grew!"

After lunch I felt a great exhaustion overcome me. I thanked Berenice and the Cantor, and expressed pleasure in seeing Hannalore again. I then excused myself and went to my room to take a nap, something I never did in the afternoons. The room was full of light, but this did not prevent me from falling asleep in my clothes. I rarely slept well at any time, but that afternoon I sank into a deep slumber that lasted three or four hours. Of course, I did not remember everything that I dreamed, but I knew I had dreamed a great deal and of many things. I felt as if I had been catching up on my dream life. What I did remember was vivid. I saw Marla and her necklace and her ashes blowing gently back into the faces of Hannalore and the Cantor while we drifted near Peche Island. I saw Bijou in Eva Moore's arms while she fed him from a teacup, and Dr. Cooley dressed as King Solomon walking through a date grove on the shore of the Sea of Galilee.

And I knew that for a long time I had dreamed of Mickey, our doctor's son, walking to his car the day of the tornado, and then of myself riding home with him to see my mother. In my waking life I had not seen Mickey for a long time. A few years before, he had gone off to college and was now living in Toronto. My parents always asked Dr. Desjarlais about his son. He would answer: "Before you know it there'll be another Dr. Desjarlais! Then I will retire."

When I was more awake from this deep slumber, I felt the wet residue of my ejaculation. I remembered seeing Mickey's body in his rain-soaked tee shirt and shorts. I removed all my clothes and put them in the hamper. I took a long shower. After I returned to my room I put on a clean shirt and shorts, and I began closing the venetian blinds on the three windows in my room. I went downstairs to my mother's sewing table to get the needle and thread with which to stitch the curtains shut. I covered the window in my bathroom with strips of duct tape I had found in a drawer in the kitchen.

I did not want to see any more sunlight. The sun, I

realized, had too much control over me. It thrust its time upon me, its signs and seasons, its days and its years, and simultaneously broke it apart so that it was disjointed and did not flow continuously. I was convinced that it disorganized my soul. I had to free myself from the sun. Still I did not intend to live in the dark. I had plenty of lamps in my room and brought an extra one up from the living room.

When I did not come down for dinner, my mother knocked on my door to see if I was all right.

"You looked very strange and tired at your party, Alexander."

It was still light outdoors. She entered my room and examined the curtains, touching them lightly with her fine hands. When she realized what I had done, for I had used a bright-red thread to sew together the blue fabric, she turned pale and left my room without another word.

My father came up a few moments later. "What have you done with the curtains, Alexander? It's still light outside. And dinner's ready."

"*Tzimtzum,*" I said. Self-contraction, retreat. God's withdrawal into Himself to make a space in which He might place the physical universe.

"*Tzimtzum?* Really? How do you expect to accomplish that?" He seemed genuinely interested but puzzled.

"I don't know yet. I'll have to see."

He suddenly laughed. "But where is there space, Alexander? You are now a solid young man!"

I pointed to my chest and then my head.

He stopped laughing. "How long do you expect it to take?"

"I don't know yet. I'll have to see."

"But Mother made dinner."

"I'd like to eat in my room."

My father shook his head doubtfully. "'*Ke haymah alu Ashshur, . . .* For they are gone up to Assyria, alone as a wild ass.'"

A short while later he came back and brought me my dinner.

What did I do the year I withdrew to my room, supposedly into myself? What was I like? I remember many things, particularly at the beginning of the process, but much of the time, time itself was a blur. In the first weeks it hung heavily around my room, like a fog unwilling to depart. And of course, this was part of the purpose. But if I ask myself why I did all this, I do not think I could give a simple unified answer. Was I trying to understand and deal with my sexual yearnings? No. I do not believe so. I had long recognized them. Somehow I had not felt shame. Shame seemed beside the point.

The first days, my mother forced herself and came regularly to visit me in my room. She rarely had anything helpful to say. She pretended to act cheerful, though this was clearly difficult for her. She had always been a serious woman. I believe she tried, however unsuccessfully and only for a short while, to trust my father's patience with me, his seeming lack of concern. She mentioned people we knew and what they had been doing.

"Hannalore has decided to stay in Windsor until the end of July. She's very lonely in Florida. And it's so hot down there in the summer. She told us she has the necklace locked up in a bank vault. It really is worth a small fortune. It has fifteen carats of emeralds and twenty of rubies! It must have once belonged to royalty!

"Yesterday Berenice and I drove Hannalore to Grosse Pointe. She wanted to see Mademoiselle Dee Dee again, but when we got to her house they told us she died last year. Remember her? I took you to see her once. She was already old then. Your father was very upset with me."

My mother attempted to orient me back into the world. For a few days she tried to engage me in similar useless conversations, though I responded only with nods and single syllables. Then one afternoon she broke down and began talking at me through her tears.

"Berenice never had any children . . . but always has a smile on her face. She never complains. Even now, with the Cantor so sick. She always tells me to count my blessings. . . . I try most of the time, I do, really, though perhaps not enough. Perhaps I've never been grateful enough—"

"And I am your punishment."

"No, Alexander. No. That's not what I meant."

But I knew better. Her visits to my room, her conversations with me, stopped.

*I*n the beginning Berenice would come to visit me. This continued only briefly, because the Cantor became more incapacitated that July.

"Are you sure you're not depressed?"

It was difficult for me not to answer her.

"I'm all right, Berenice, really."

"It sometimes happens to teenagers. It's a difficult time. It's hard to figure out who one is and what one should do. Depression is nothing to be ashamed of. When I was—"

"I'm all right, Berenice. I'm not depressed." I looked her in the eye. "And I'm not ashamed of anything, either."

"Well, Alexander, if you say so, I believe you. I just don't understand."

My father, after several days, when he realized I was serious about my isolation, insisted on getting me a small air conditioner. "Don't worry. It won't let in any light. But it's unhealthy to stay in here with no air."

I kept my room meticulously clean, and this took up a fair amount of my time. I swept the floor whenever I woke up from sleep. Once a day I scrubbed the sink, the shower stall, the toilet. I dusted all the surfaces of the room: my desk, the windowsills, the headboard of my bed.

At night, when the sun did not rule, I made excursions into the house, mostly to my father's library. Every night for the first week of my retreat, I took my great-grandfather's book out of its little glass sarcophagus, turning the tiny silver key in the miniature silver lock. I had never before attempted to read it.

I struggled at first with the Gothic script but was quickly able to decipher it with a handbook of my father's. It was an annoying script, since so many of the letters were practically identical. I slowly rewrote the German into modern script in an empty notebook, until I became accustomed to the old lettering. I looked up many old-fashioned words and expressions that I didn't know in the dictionary.

It was a great struggle for what was, I was shocked to learn, an unscholarly and self-absorbed book. My great-grandfather had left his wife and three-year-old daughter, my father's mother, for the noble purpose, as the title would have one believe, of traveling in the footsteps of Abraham. But his slender account in a stiff *Hochdeutsch* concerned itself mostly with his initial stormy sea voyage from Hamburg to Tyre and, as he delicately put it, his *Verdauungsstörung*, his indigestion. There were other discomforts he suffered traveling overland, through the Syrian desert, past the site of ancient Palmyra, to the Euphrates. Further humiliations awaited him when he sailed down that miasmic river in the entourage of a barbaric prince who, despite his handsome and imposing figure, picked his nose publicly and would not sit still for his lessons.

Though my great-grandfather witnessed many strange customs of the local people, he did not elaborate on them. There was little discussion of the splendid geography that spread out before him or the sites of the ancient cities or academies of Babylonia that had so fascinated my father. And there was no further reference to Abraham after the title page!

I had, as a result of reading my great-grandfather's book, improved certain aspects of my German grammar, particularly the dative and genitive forms.

I then undertook to study the Ugaritic language, a forerunner of the Kana'anite dialects and Hebrew. My father had been studying an introductory text by the famous scholar Cassuto about the Goddess Anat, and I taught myself the cuneiform markings that wedged themselves into a variety of small constellations. If God had indeed created the world from words, I was determined, as my father had been, to see where these words came from. My father must have noticed that I had pulled this book from his shelf. Perhaps I put it back in the wrong place. The next night I found on his desk a new edition, with the complete photographs of the Ras Shamrah tablets discovered by Villoreaud and the entire known text of the Ugaritic myths. I deciphered the fragmented story of the ancient gods, of Mot, of Asherah, of Baal and his warrior sister, Anat. I also read a book that had caught my night-wandering eyes, *Physics and the Laws of Thermodynamics*, which my father had in his library.

Eventually and I suppose inevitably, I myself became an object of study. Every morning at dawn I locked my door and went into my bathroom and took a long shower. Then I stood and examined the container of my soul carefully in the closet mirror. I studied every square inch of my skin with a magnifying glass and scrutinized my back with the additional help of a pocket mirror. I felt and caressed every muscle and palpable bone. In the encyclopedia, I read up on what I saw or thought I saw. I delved deeper than my mere sensual surface anatomy, below the skin and the contours of muscles and bone. I read about the nourishing arteries and the veins that run like a sieve through our entire bodies. I tried to imagine this great wave of fluid that washed continually through our corporeal selves, that was our very essence.

I began reading about the brain. I learned the six cell layers of the cerebral cortex, its surface geography, with the names of the convolutions and fissures. One night I left a small slip of colored paper to mark the place in the encyclopedia that I was reading, between the pages on the cerebellum and the cerebral hemispheres. The next night I found books on related topics lying on the bench of the birdcage, textbooks of neuroanatomy and neurophysiology that my father had brought me from the public library. Whenever I was interested in a subject I left another slip of paper in a book, and the next night I would find a more thorough treatise on the topic lying on the bench in the birdcage.

We never discussed this strange papery dialogue of requested information and delivered books during the ritual of afternoon visits my father had begun to make to my room. My father never referred to them, and I rarely spoke. I believe this gave my father hope and the patience to see me through the time of my isolation. If I was reading and learning, he believed, I would no doubt return safely to the sunlit workaday world.

I spent the better part of July reading about the nervous pathways that flowed from the brain's surface to the very surface of the body, to the edge of its own little universe and the border of the unknown. I felt I could see the great axonal network that housed our souls and wove our dreams.

And so my days and nights were filled. I had developed a routine. I began to sleep only when I was tired, usually during the daylight hours, after my shower and self-scrutiny at dawn. I woke up in the late afternoons, when my father came to visit me. At night I read.

I dreamed many strange dreams that year and wrote them in a notebook. My dream book was written in my own code, a backward Ugaritic that I myself can no longer read, so that my parents would not try to decipher it. Sometimes I dreamed I was locked in a dark space, holding a door shut with all my strength while vicious dogs or monsters waited outside to get me. The air in this space would run out and I would awake in a terrible sweat, gasping for breath. Other times I dreamed of Mickey, and he would be holding me tightly. "Don't worry," he would say, kissing me softly, exploring the parts of my body that I myself had discovered and learned about in my readings. "Don't worry. Don't worry. My father says the Rabbi's wife will be fine. . . . I love you. . . . You're a wonderful man. . . ." Whenever I dreamed about Mickey I woke up and felt the wetness below. I would then get up and shower for a long time. Still I looked forward to these dreams and never felt ashamed.

———

One afternoon while I was sleeping my mother knocked loudly on my bedroom door.

"Mrs. Cook is here, Alexander. Please wake up and get dressed."

I quickly dressed and stood in my doorway. I had not seen Mrs. Cook in the months since Marla's funeral. She wore her usual black and looked the same as she always had. She even had the same pearl necklace around her collar.

"Marla came to me three times in the last week, always whispering in my ear. My daughter is as insistent in death as she was in life. She asked me to give you this."

Mrs. Cook handed me a small blue velvet pouch. She watched me intently as I withdrew its contents. Inside was a large sapphire set in silver, the one Marla had worn pinned to a red headband when I visited her at Texas Children's Hospital.

"I don't know why she wanted you to have it so badly just now, but she did. I'm glad, though, really. It shows she still has the most generous soul. If you thank her I know she will hear you."

"Thank you, Marla," I said so Mrs. Cook would hear me. "Thank you."

For a moment I wanted to ask Mrs. Cook if this beautiful jewel actually saved a life, or perhaps several, but I decided not to say any more. Perhaps I did not want to take the chance and find out that it hadn't saved anyone. I wanted to believe that it had.

After that I wore the sapphire all the time, even when I showered, suspended from my neck on a simple piece of string.

Crown Heights

I do not know when my father began his "magnum opus," his "sandstone ziggurat," any more than I know precisely when my mother began to worry obsessively about me, though clearly he began contemplating this huge labor before I reached the age of awareness. It was always there in my childhood, in its manifold manifestations and potentialities: the great map on the study wall with its colored flag pins and jagged lines, the endless volumes and tomes, the notebooks, the piles of exotic correspondence, even the Sefirotic Tree.

I do not know if there was any connection between the

independent obsessions of my parents: my mother's uncontrollable fears and my father's unanswerable intellectual and spiritual pursuits. Does the owner of one obsession attract another? I am at a loss to explain such an association, or what it could be, yet somehow feel there was a thread I have not uncovered. I no longer have anyone to ask.

I do know that my father was never able to finish any of his books, perhaps because he returned to his sources over and over and was never satisfied, was always reexamining and reevaluating his main theories.

I have come to believe that this endless and fruitless process itself replaced his original goal, whatever it was, usurping the real purpose of his research. His other overwhelming interests, the structure of the Godhead, the primordial, universe-enabling *Ursprache,* and his need to integrate and unify all his various ideas and theories, only served to confuse him more, to hold him further from his ostensible aims. I am amazed that despite all this, despite all his eccentricities of thought and pursuit, he never went mad. He did not walk around a frustrated or an angry man, a latter-day Faust. He did manage, though, to publish several articles, and perhaps this kept him sane. To the end, my father remained the most stable force in my life.

Though my father could not integrate his yearnings toward unknowable knowledge, he tried explaining them to me in the daily conversations or, more precisely, the monologues he established during my inner change and my rejection of the rule of solar time. He saw what was happening to me and tried to reach me. Perhaps he had similar difficulties himself, though I do not know; he never mentioned it directly.

During the first week of my *tzimtzum* and retreat into my bedroom, when he realized I was determined to remain there, my father began visiting me every afternoon. I suppose these visits were his own attempts at my therapy. He believed, no doubt, that the discussion of his lifelong work might have some bearing on my situation, on what was plaguing me. Perhaps, though, he did not know what else to talk about. At the beginning of my seclusion, he once, and only once, said, "Your mother thinks you should be sent away somewhere, to an institution, where they can treat you and get you better, but I do not agree with her. I do not believe in mind doctors who practice methods with no empirical proof. And I do not believe you are really sick. Your mother has always had her own uncontrollable fears." He smiled. "Perhaps you've noticed. But she has learned to control if not conquer them without the help of such doctors or their harmful 'treatments.' Anyway, Alexander, since you are still a rational being you must work things out for yourself, at your own pace."

My father explained many things during his visits. One afternoon he spoke quite heatedly. "What matters is not a city's or a person's physical location, of course, because physical place is only temporary, a function of the earth's continuous motion in the heavens, through a hurtling galaxy. Place, Alexander, is an illusion, a manifestation of God's imagination and a function of Time. As you grow older you may find that Windsor will be another place than it is now"—a droplet of moisture glimmered at the corner of his mouth—"and we will be different people than we are now, too. For we are ourselves encapsulated spaces, containers for the soul."

He often repeated his theory of time and place, in which he borrowed heavily from kabbalistic writings and a knowledge of physics. Sometimes he spoke in a lowered voice, not the clear, well-modulated voice, that captivating voice, which always carried his sermon across the grand sanctuary of our synagogue. Sitting near my bed, he almost whispered. "If Time were abolished, so would Place be, and the Laws of Thermodynamics, and so would God. Therefore, of course, none of this can ever happen. And that knowledge, that certainty, is what keeps me going. This understanding is especially important for us, Alexander, and especially in these places in which we live nowadays. These places which still somehow frighten us. Isn't that part of what keeps you in here?"

"No."

He paid no attention to my answer and continued his discourse:

"Our forefathers, strangely enough—and this I believe is the real root of mankind's problem—originally came not from Kana'an, not from an earthly Jerusalem, but from the far Euphrates with its source in Eden, from an impossibly remote and primordial home. We cannot forget it, or ever find it again. I believe this fact has afflicted us to the present day."

*I*n the middle of summer, in the sixth or seventh week of my retreat, my father took me on a pilgrimage. He actually called it that himself. Except for that excursion and a few remarkable others, I would continue to remain in my room and our house for almost a year. Only after my parents were asleep would I venture from my room. Before going into my father's library, I would look out the various windows of the darkened house to the night contours of our neighborhood. Night joined everything together.

I learned to watch and appreciate the moon. The moon amazed and comforted me. She changed herself slowly, at her own pace. She grew wide and looming and then gradually diminished herself and withdrew. In her profound humility, she imitated the submissive tides that she ruled.

When I was younger my father explained the sad fate of the moon. "In the beginning the moon was as brilliant as the sun. Together they amazed the world with their light. But the moon complained to God: 'How can two rule the sky?' So God punished the moon and set her to rule over the night."

"And what about the stars?"

"God regretted that He punished the moon, and so He set the stars in attendance to appease her."

I did not expect my situation, my isolation and withdrawal, to go on forever, but I was determined to endure it as long as need be. I knew I had a stubborn heart and could continue in this solitary state until I was ready to leave it.

I had few visitors besides my father. My mother would pass by my room several times a day, knock, and leave my meals at the door. She did not speak to me much. She took me at my word and viewed me as a punishment. If she had to, my mother would bear this new punishment in silence, as she had her other punishments. I realized that this was how she viewed all her life's disappointments. It was no doubt a torment for her to remain silent. I understood that from the time she revealed her feelings, when she argued with my father and said, "I've been punished enough. How many of *my* selves, my babies, died over the years?" When she finally said what she had been waiting years to say.

Berenice at first came to see me often, but after a month or so it was clear to everyone that the Cantor was dying. Berenice had to spend more and more time tending him.

Though it would take him many months to die, time was not on their side and became their enemy too.

The Cantor could no longer get out of bed, and Berenice hardly left her house. Sometimes if she had errands to do she might let my mother stay with the Cantor for an hour or so, but more often she let my mother and father do her shopping for her. She refused to have any nurses or aides help her take care of her husband.

She explained to me on one of her last visits that summer: "I once told you why, Alexander, remember? When something bad happens to the person you love, you must never leave him. Even if it seems unbearable to be with him and watch him suffer. Otherwise it is like you are setting yourself up as a judge and punishing the victim. It's not their fault that they are victims. I've talked to your father about it many times, and he always agrees with me. I think you know that, and you learned that, too, from Marla and Mrs. Cook." She thought for a moment, then added: "I try never to give up a single minute with him. You can never bring back a single lost second."

"And you can never take back a single spoken word," I said.

Berenice looked at me, puzzled, waiting for an explanation, but I returned to silence.

My father corresponded for many years with a scholar in Brooklyn, New York, Dr. Avram Aschenbach. He sometimes referred to him as "my friend Dr. Mahuza," because Dr. Aschenbach's specialty was that same ancient city on the Fluvius Regum, the Royal River, which became a center of study after the destruction of Nehardea and where the great sage Rava headed the academy for fourteen years.

I did not think my father had anyone whom he could really call a friend, not in the way other people say they have friends. He had no one in whom he could confide his most personal concerns. I suppose I am like him in this way. But in his case perhaps this was on account of his profession. People were always coming to him with their problems, and he was supposed to have all the answers. On the other hand, he never acted as if he had all the answers; he just did his best to understand a situation that was presented to him.

"I am only a middleman for each unique and personal heart," he would say. "I am merely a sounding board. Most people find the answers they need within themselves."

When speaking of my father's capacity for friendship, I am not, of course, trying to sidestep the issue or exclude from the category of friendship the Cantor and Berenice, who were so bound up with his rabbinical and spiritual life and with our family. They were indeed his friends, and he would be the first to say, "They are my dearest friends," but I have no evidence that he ever turned to the Cantor or Berenice in a moment of great personal concern. There is no evidence I can infer of him seeking their confidence or pouring his heart out to them. Perhaps he did not dare. I think, however, he tried to learn from both of them, from the Cantor's Job-like sufferings and from Berenice's enduring and persistent love.

My father, though, after all the years of correspondence with Dr. Maḥuza, began confiding in him as one would a friend. He told him about me, his troubled son. Dr. Maḥuza, or Dr. Avram Aschenbach, was a staunch follower of a Hasidic rebbe.

"The Rebbe is better than any psychologist or psychiatrist," he wrote my father in a letter I discovered after my father's death. "Maybe he can help your boy." My father clearly came from a background light-years away from the communities and beliefs of the Hasidim. Their figureheads had never played a role in his life or in the religious training he sought for himself to the horror of his parents. They were as foreign to him as he was to his parents' unshakable unbelief. I cannot recall his mentioning this or that rebbe at any time during my childhood, except in the case of Dr. Avram Aschenbach and only as the Aramaic expression goes, *agav urḥa*—on the way, in passing reference.

One afternoon in the middle of summer, in the month of Tammuz, the Sumerian-derived name of the fourth lunar month, my father came into my room for his daily visit. "Alexander, would you like to go on a trip? A little pilgrimage?" I didn't answer him at first. I did not always answer his questions. He asked me again: "Would you like to go see the Rebbe? My friend Dr. Mahuza thinks it might be good for you. He can easily arrange it. It's usually very hard to see the Rebbe. He's a very wise man."

I said no.

Several days passed. Each afternoon my father came into the room and eventually, between talk of his theories, asked me the same question. "Would you like to go with me and see the Rebbe?"

One night when I ventured out of my room to my father's library, I overheard my parents arguing in their bedroom. It was about midnight. I had rarely heard them argue at any time, except on that occasion before my grandfather's death, when my mother brought the telegram from Frankfurt to my father's library.

I stood just outside their bedroom door. My mother was saying, "It's no different than going to that fortune-teller in Grosse Pointe, which upset you so much all those years ago. You made me feel ashamed. And I confess you were right to do so, but now you're being a fool!"

My father said, "It's not the same, Sarah, God forbid the comparison. He's a holy man, not a fortune-teller; maybe he can help or advise us."

"You should be taking him to a doctor. He needs drastic treatment before he gets worse, something—maybe electric- or insulin-shock therapy. There are new techniques available. I've been reading all about them. They *do* work.

He doesn't need some phony miracle worker or any pseudo-religious hocus-pocus!"

There was a pause, and I knew my father was carefully considering his answer.

"Sarah, please. Mind what you say about such a holy man." My father spoke firmly. "I will not and cannot force Alexander, but if he agrees to go see the Rebbe, I'm taking him."

The next day when my father came into the room, before he asked me again, I announced, "I'll go if we can come back the same day." Though I had decided to go, I could not imagine passing the night in any room other than my bedroom or in any house other than our own.

My father broke into a broad and beautiful smile. I never before gave much thought to my father's appearance, I never allowed myself to contemplate it, to travel that dangerous avenue of thought. But at that moment I calmly saw how handsome he was, with his noble face, his thick black hair, and his fine tall figure. Perhaps that was why my mother married him even after being rejected by his parents. Perhaps that's why she continued to love him despite the distractions of her pathological fears.

My father didn't waste any time. I suppose he was afraid I would change my mind or was afraid my mother would do something to prevent us. But she didn't. Strangely, it was she who came in and woke me early the next morning.

"Alexander, wake up. You'll miss your airplane."

My father then came into my room and had me put on a white shirt, tie, and jacket. My clothes had begun to fit a little too tightly.

"You've managed to grow like one of those tropical plants that thrive in the shade of the rain forests! Well, that's fine. You look fine. You can't visit the Rebbe without being dressed properly. It would be disrespectful."

As soon as I was dressed we drove to Detroit via the tunnel. It was a warm August morning, and we continued on to the airport for the flight to New York. My father parked the car in the day lot. "It's amazing how one can travel so far in one day," he said. "It makes you think. Such a great distance in one day and then back in your own home and bed."

When we arrived in New York, Dr. Aschenbach was waiting at the terminal. He was a small, wiry man with a black goatee. The two men had never seen each other before despite their years of correspondence.

They recognized one another instantly. Dr. Aschenbach walked right up to my father and said, "Rav Shelomo?" He then said hello to me.

As we drove to Crown Heights in Dr. Aschenbach's old car, the two scholars spoke of their mutual interests. Dr. Aschenbach had received a visa to travel to Iraq to visit the site of Mahuza.

"Oh, I'll find it," he told my father. "Nowadays it's a short trip from Baghdad. But it wasn't easy getting permission from their government. It's only because they know about our Rebbe and respect him. The whole world does, even the Iraqis. I have a guide arranged there and everything." He told my father that the Rebbe had given him his blessing, which he believed would guarantee his success.

My father told him—no doubt something he had already done in their correspondence—how his own grandfather, at the turn of the century, had left his home in Frankfurt to travel along the Euphrates in the company of an exiled Persian prince.

"It was a dangerous and difficult proposition then, what with all the diseases and epidemics."

"Yes, of course," Dr. Aschenbach said. "Even nowadays one needs several shots."

My father opened his briefcase and tried to hand Dr. Aschenbach his treasured copy of *Auf den Spuren Abrahams entlang des Euphrat.*

"Here, take this with you."

"Oh, no, I couldn't." Dr. Aschenbach waved his free hand, holding the steering wheel with the other. "Never, never, never. It's too valuable. It might get lost or stolen."

My father kept insisting. "Please, take it. It will be as if my grandfather is traveling with you. Please, he would have loved the idea."

Dr. Aschenbach finally gave in and accepted the slender leather-bound book. He placed it on his lap. "With God's help, I will return it to you safely when I get back."

*D*r. Aschenbach drove us past the house where the Rebbe lived. The wide avenue was lined with majestic old trees that stretched up and curved overhead to form an endless cathedral-like canopy in the summer afternoon. As we drove along I was reminded of the broad tree-lined Lake Shore Drive. The houses here were also enormous, like mansions, but unlike those in Grosse Pointe, they stood crowded together and there was no lake to be seen. And here on the street, the men for the most part dressed darkly, in long black robes over their black pants. The women wore awkward-looking wigs covered with old-fashioned hats. I had never seen such people before.

We then drove around the corner to the building where the Rebbe held his interviews. The anteroom of the Rebbe's office was jammed with other people: childless couples who were seeking the Rebbe's blessing; parents with children who were clearly retarded or deformed. A little girl with heavy braces on her legs stared at me the whole time. I thought of Marla, that perhaps she should have come here. There were also men and women who simply sought some personal advice from their spiritual leader.

After twenty minutes or so of waiting, Dr. Aschenbach spoke to the secretary and gestured toward my father and myself. Dr. Aschenbach frowned, rolled his eyes, pointed to his watch, then to the ceiling.

It wasn't long before we were ushered into the Rebbe's office. It was a small, sunny room, sparsely furnished, with a simple wooden desk. The Rebbe sat behind it. Four stained-glass windows gave onto the parkway. In the right window was a slender pink tulip, and in the far left window, an owl seated on its branch. Dr. Aschenbach handed an assistant a slip of paper, which the assistant in turn handed to the Rebbe, who quickly glanced at it. The Rebbe was then already in his sixties, with a gray-black beard and blue eyes. He looked up at us. My father extended his hand, and the Rebbe rose and took it. The Rebbe then shook Dr. Aschenbach's hand and, lastly, mine. His hand was large and soft. He did not ask us any questions. He looked directly at me for what seemed a long while and smiled. I was surprised when he began speaking. He spoke perfect English, with no accent. My father just stood there, watching and listening, his mouth slightly open.

"It's not always as hopeless as one may think, Aryeh Alexander, though I do not presume to read your mind— that is God's province, and true prophecy has been weakened since the destruction of the Temples. But you should know that women often have greater wisdom than men and that is where true beauty resides. That is why the Divine Shekhinah, God's Presence in our world, is always compared to a woman, a mother, and a wife, though this is only a simplification, a way for the human mind to understand what cannot be understood. The Shekhinah followed Adam and Eve out of Eden, and the Shekhinah follows all of us in our time of Exile to provide us with a home. She is with us in our waking hours and escorts our souls when we dream. She suffers when She sees our lonely suffering, and She rejoices in our happiness." He stared at me a moment with his blue eyes. "Do you understand? It is Her love we must seek. She is never isolated from us."

The Rebbe turned and nodded to his assistant. Our meeting was over.

As we were being ushered out of the small room, I stopped for a moment near the doorway. I stood transfixed. The stained-glass owl was projected by a dense shaft of sunlight onto the parquet floor before me. It had in this new manifestation become larger, more brilliant and colorful. I was startled because for a moment I thought it spoke to me, but then the shaft of light with its image faded, and I realized the Rebbe was speaking: "That is a beautiful gem you are wearing under your shirt, Aryeh Alexander. A sapphire? I can see the blue peeking out. Our father Abraham was a very wealthy man and wore a precious jewel around his neck. All who looked upon it were healed.

But still, you must take care of your health, especially your ears."

On the flight back to Detroit, as the plane made its ascent, my father kept repeating softly, "Of course, the Shekhinah, the Shekhinah. It is so simple. She follows us everywhere. She *becomes* every place and *makes* it our home." He was clearly struck by the Rebbe's words and found an important message in them for himself.

Suddenly I heard a strange popping sound. The interior of the airplane began to spin, and I screamed out, thinking we were going to crash.

"We're not going to crash, Alexander. We're not going to crash," my father kept saying.

I closed my eyes, and I kept screaming because I still felt us spinning. Several stewardesses, and eventually the copilot, had to come over to reassure me. "You are just dizzy," the copilot said. He then held my head steadily between his two strong hands. "You're just a bit dizzy, young man. It happens sometimes in airplanes. Keep your eyes closed for now." He said to my father, "You'd better take him to a doctor as soon as we land."

Later I learned that the membranous covering of my inner ear, the round window of my cochlea, had broken, causing an attack of vertigo and leaving me permanently deaf in the left ear.

When the plane landed in Detroit my father was frantic. He wanted to take me immediately to a local hospital, since the hospitals in Detroit were bigger than in Windsor, but as we drove on the highway downtown to Ford Hospital, the whole city was ablaze.

"My God! What's going on! It's like the End of Days. It's like the End of Days!" my father kept saying. When he turned on the radio we learned that riots had broken out. The National Guard had been called in. Great mushroom clouds of fire and smoke burst up where neighborhoods and gas stations once stood. My father drove erratically, swerving from lane to lane whenever he heard an explosion. I grasped my sapphire, but this did not help my increasing nausea. I vomited on myself. We had to make our way to the Canadian border, to the tunnel and the safety of our home.

My father was so shaken when we arrived at the house that he was gasping for breath. My mother had been beside herself with worry. "Thank God you made it! Thank God you made it home. Detroit is burning up!" She held on to my father for several minutes before she would let him go.

When they both calmed down my father called Dr. Desjarlais. He had us meet him at Hôtel-Dieu. After he examined me he called in an ear specialist.

"There's not much anyone can do when this happens," the specialist said. He looked at me and then at my parents. "Fortunately his other ear is perfect. He may be dizzy for a few days until he gets his equilibrium back. He should rest and stay in bed and keep his eyes closed." And then he added: "It's wonderful to rise above the clouds and see the sun or the stars, but maybe the young man should avoid flying in the future."

When we drove home from Hôtel-Dieu, my mother said, "Well, what did the Rebbe say?"

My father was completely exhausted. "The Rebbe? Oh, later, Sarah, later. I can barely think."

The Sun at Home

One spring morning when I was small, my father and mother woke me before dawn.

"Hurry, Alexander, get dressed," my father said. "Who knows if we will ever again merit to witness such an event. You, Alexander, no doubt will, but your mother and I are older."

I quickly got dressed, and then we walked the three blocks to the synagogue in the dark. The Cantor, a sleepy, eye-rubbing Berenice, and several members of the congregation were already gathering outdoors on the broad stairway of the synagogue. The sky was clear, and the air was still cool from the vanishing night. A lonely morning star shone above the horizon.

My father gave a small sermon: "In every generation, our Sages tell us, the Sun returns to the place of his brilliant birth and realigns in the firmament as at Creation. Through all the millennia, the pilgrim Sun has never forgotten the glory of his home. And so we, too, must never forget our homes and those who are always there to love us. And we must never forget the glory of our eternal home, Jerusalem."

As the sun rose over the neat low houses that stood opposite the synagogue, my father lifted me in his arms to make sure I could see. It was the first time I saw a sunrise. My mother stood next to us. The Cantor led the congregation in the blessing of the sun, "Blessed are You Who makes the works of Creation." He then sang the most beautiful melody I had ever heard, a melody he himself had composed, "Praise Him Sun and Moon, Praise Him All You Stars of Light." I looked around and saw that people were crying from the sheer beauty of the song and the wonder of a moment that came so rarely in any lifetime. My father kept whispering in my ear, "Just listen, Alexander. Okay? Just listen."

Years later, when the Cantor was dying, at the time of my *tzimtzum*, I begged him to sing me that melody. For some reason I became obsessed with it after I returned from my pilgrimage to the Rebbe and lost the hearing in my left ear. I seemed always to hear the melody faintly in the dimness of my room. I heard it indistinctly, with crucial notes missing, as through a tightly closed door. I believed without a doubt that within the pattern of its notes it held a corresponding light, and the secret to my restoration and redemption. I could not help myself. I walked next door after dark.

At that time Berenice had strict orders from the doctor to limit visitors. But she was so surprised and encouraged that I had taken the initiative to walk out of my house and go over to hers after so many months that I easily persuaded her to allow me a moment or two with the Cantor, even though it was getting late and he had been sleeping.

"I only have a small question I need to ask him. About music."

"I know the Cantor will be happy to see you."

She went into the bedroom and gently woke him. The room smelled of antiseptic.

"Alexander is here, Bernhard, Alexander is here."

Without so much as a 'How are you?' I quoted the words from the Psalm, hoping to remind the waking Cantor of his melody "Praise Him Sun and Moon, Praise Him All You Stars of Light."

He lifted his head weakly off his pillow. "Alexander, is that you?" His face was even smoother and rounder than before, slightly puffy around the eyelids.

"Yes. Yes. Can't you remember it anymore, Cantor? You composed it yourself, didn't you?"

His languages now became confused. He had trouble breathing. "What? Remember *was*? *Oui, oui.* Oh, no. . . . *Ich kann mich nicht rememberen.*"

"Didn't you write it down somewhere?"

"I can't remember anymore. *Kannst du mir singen?* Are you a tenor *oder ein Bass?*"

"No. I can't sing. How could you forget? You wrote it!" I sensed my voice shaking, losing control. I was gripped with a terrible fear that I was losing my very self. I could not tell if I was laughing or crying.

And then I took in a long breath and was able to control myself somewhat. "How could you forget, Cantor? How could you? It was so beautiful!"

He turned his head away from me, and I was shocked when I noticed how skinny and curved his neck had become, like a newborn bird's. I could see all the tendons, the vertebrae, his jutting voice box. His arteries fluttered under the skin. He began babbling a list of names. "Elchanan. . . . Lotte. . . . Richard. . . . Tosca . . ."

I felt faint. Berenice came forward in the room. She took my arm gently and led me away. She had changed over the time of the Cantor's illness. She had grown thin, tired-looking; her hair was streaked with gray. She seemed to have taken upon herself the years of her husband, who looked more and more like a baby as he lay dying on his bed. She spoke softly and kindly, for she always loved me very much. "Alexander, the Cantor is so tired. Let's let him rest. But if you had loved the music so much, what made you laugh?"

"But I didn't laugh. I just asked—"

Berenice said sadly, "No, Alexander, you did laugh. Long ago, on the synagogue stairs. You were only a child; maybe you don't remember. Your father had to hush you, you were acting so strangely. I think that's when your mother began worrying about you, though I never understood why she was so upset. Children sometimes act funny for no reason. I told her maybe you were still half asleep— it was so early—and laughing in your sleep. But I knew you weren't sleeping." She paused, looking carefully at me. "I guess it doesn't matter anymore. It was so long ago. Maybe later we'll ask the Cantor again, when he gets his strength back. Maybe he'll remember his music."

The Cantor never did get his strength back. Though he lived many more months, I never saw him again.

The following spring when my mother came into my room to tell me that the Cantor had died, I said nothing but ran to one of my windows. I raised its curtains, which had been sewn together, and the blind that had been drawn closed for almost a year. I peeked out on the brilliant noonday world and felt a great relief. For in my grief, I thought the sun had died.

Sha'arai Rakhamim

I did not go to the Cantor's funeral. This was, as it turned out, not on account of my seclusion. I was already preparing myself to leave it. I had already, when I heard of the Cantor's death, for a moment raised the curtains and blinds in my room and looked out at the noonday sun for the first time in almost a year.

I did not go because I was experiencing sudden renewed attacks of vertigo. I had not slept in the twenty-four hours since my mother told me of the Cantor's death. I lay in my bed wide awake. I wanted desperately to go to his funeral to say good-bye to him. I thought it might jog my memory, too, and help me remember the melody he sang all those years before: "Praise Him Sun and Moon, Praise Him All You Stars of Light." But when I tried sitting up in bed the room began spinning. And while the room spun about its axis, I looked down as if from a great height and saw myself lying below in my bed. I saw myself clearly. I saw that my eyes were closed. I was holding on to the edges of the headboard with my arms stretched backward. I saw myself as I was then, a young man lying in bed in a white tee shirt and jeans. I saw the sapphire I wore around my neck, and my long hair, which had not been cut in almost a year, arranged around my head like a dark pool. My legs were stretched out to the foot of the bed. This attack with all its strange visual perceptions was different and worse than my initial vertigo all those months before, when I felt the airplane spiraling out of control, when the specialist had said my equilibrium would get better.

As the room spun about me and I above the room, I encountered myself. And though I cannot say I was displeased with this encounter—for I felt a warm sense of pleasure at the sight of my man's body lying there on the bed—I was also terrified.

When my parents came home the new attack had subsided, though I was still somewhat dizzy.

My father told me that Hannalore had been at the funeral but looked unwell. "There is no life in her anymore."

And it turned out to be true, because Hannalore died several weeks after the Cantor, near the end of spring. Her body was flown back from Key West, to which she had briefly returned. She was buried in Windsor, next to her brother, at the Sha'arai Rakhamim, the Gates of Mercy cemetery.

A brief letter addressed to my father accompanied her will.

Dear Rabbi,

I hope you will allow me to be buried in your cemetery with my crucifix. I know you are a wise man and have always known it means more to me than two toy sticks hitting each other over their heads. I understand that there can be no Christian marking on my tombstone. Please let me be buried next to my brother.

Sincerely,
Hannalore Seidengarn

My father did nothing to prevent Hannalore's burial in the synagogue's cemetery.

"No one will ever see her crucifix again," he told me. "I suppose I will even miss it a little. It had become a part of her. It gave her courage, and so, despite everything, one must look upon that as a good thing."

I did not go to Hannalore's funeral either, because I still did not feel well enough. After my renewed attack of vertigo on the day of the Cantor's funeral, I suppose I understood that I was not yet ready to leave my period of withdrawal.

Before they left for the cemetery for Hannalore's funeral, my mother and Berenice had come to my room. Perhaps Berenice had asked my mother to come in with her, for my mother seemed reluctant to enter. Both friends were dressed in black. Berenice had continued to lose weight, and though she was still much taller than my mother, the two women began to resemble each other more than they ever really had in the days when they would come home with the same hairdos, giggling, when my father and the Cantor would call them the Bobbsey Twins.

I said I couldn't go to the cemetery. I was sorry.

Berenice said that it would be as if I had been there anyway. "I want you to know that both Hannalore and the Cantor understand."

"It's impossible for them to understand," I said. "They're dead. Present tense. Eternal tense. Dead." I said this flatly, without emotion, without malice or anger, just as I had had no malice or anger in me when I said to my mother, "And I am your punishment." I said this because I believed it was true, for where was the vaporous soul when its vault had been destroyed? I had begun to realize in my period of study and seclusion that our souls were no more lasting or real than the watery matrix of our bodies. All that mattered to me was the clear statement, the unobstructed, even if tormenting, truth. I had recently seen myself as I was then, a young man lying in bed, holding on for dear life.

Berenice said: "No, you're wrong, Alexander. They both do love you and they do understand. 'Present tense. Eternal tense.'"

I did not answer her with words but nodded once or twice, because what she now said appeared true. I turned away in my bed as they left the room.

One month later, days before the unveiling of Hannalore's tombstone, I felt myself becoming better. My vertigo was completely gone. I had begun walking around the house during the daytime but had not yet gone outside.

The night before the unveiling, Berenice came over and visited me.

I said I wanted to go to the unveiling.

Berenice thought I should stay home.

"You can go another time. The stone will always be there. The main thing is that you remember Hannalore in your heart and perhaps think of her from time to time so that she has an afterlife in you—in case you are right and she is really as dead as you said and there is no afterlife." Berenice became agitated and pulled at her fingers. "I cannot dare to think like that, Alexander. I cannot think like you do. I have no choice. I cannot afford that luxury. Otherwise where would the Cantor or Hannalore be after all they suffered?"

But I did not want merely to remember Hannalore in my heart so that she might have an afterlife in me. I wanted to come back to the world with its ungovernable, unrestrainable time, even though it might include as part of the world the part that was death.

The next day I woke up before dawn, before my parents or Berenice. I showered quickly and got dressed. I waited patiently on the front porch in the morning light.

I rode to the cemetery with Berenice and my parents for Hannalore's unveiling.

When the cover was withdrawn from the stone, I read the inscription. Hannalore's name was carved on top in English. As I read it I heard her own voice whispering, reading out her name to me. "Hannalore Seidengarn!"

It was a strange name really, Seidengarn: a ball of silken yarn. In one of the fairy tales my father used to read me, there was a king who had a magic ball of yarn. If he got lost the yarn would unravel itself and show him the way through the dark forest.

I thought it funny to hear Hannalore speak her name now that she was dead. Her voice did not convince me then that there was an afterlife or a wandering of souls, because I did not know where her voice came from. I did not know if it came from a wandering soul or a soul calling down from the afterlife. I realized the voice might have come from within me. Perhaps her soul had even entered mine. I had read somewhere, in one of my father's kabbalistic tracts, that this could happen. Departing souls would try to cling to those of the living but were always torn away. There was finally no strength in them. They were no match for a bound-up-in-life soul.

Hannalore did not stop with this deep and smoke-clouded recitation of her name but insisted on reminding my mother of something she had told her long ago, in words that took on new meaning. I could not tell if my mother heard her, for Hannalore had continued in a whisper. "C'est vrai, Madame Rabbi. I tell you this woman has said such things about my very self, no one else could have known them."

And then Hannalore said, "C'est notre petit secret!"

And while she spoke I looked underneath the English lettering to the small Hebrew inscription that contained the same honeyed letters that God used to create His universe in seven days: Ud mutzal m'aish. "An ember saved from the fire."

Then I read Hannalore's Hebrew name: "Elchanan ben David." Elchanan son of David.

I think now of this stone inscription, of how quickly our minds assemble the symbols that are our written language.

I see quickly the full words, a man's name, the son of another man. But at that time it seemed I was reading everything slowly, letter by individual letter, until the ember spared from fire floated before me, burning brightly, phosphorescent like the letters I used to imagine at Creation. The name itself became a little holy universe suspended before me, containing components of my own name as well. And it seemed I was reading for such a long time that nowadays, when I look back, I cannot account for that slow passage of time. It seemed to me then that several minutes, maybe hours, went by as I read and as I overheard Hannalore speak.

And yet what I also remember and what came to me suddenly was my mother's screams, in her own and different flow of time, as the stone was uncovered and she herself made out the inscription.

She looked briefly at me, wide-eyed, while Hannalore spoke. My mother began screaming in a high, unnatural voice that resembled no sound I had ever heard from her modest frame, nor any sound I could otherwise imagine coming from any human being. And she went from this screaming into a long protracted weeping that frightened me more than the weeping I eavesdropped on that day so many years before when the two children on Tecumseh Road were killed. But this time I did not laugh in fear as I had done long ago in my hiding place when I witnessed the cries of the parents and the weeping of my mother. And I remembered without remorse but with a simple and clear recognition how I had laughed then.

As my mother wept, she flailed her arms through the air and began beating herself on the head. My father tried to grab hold of one of her arms, and she accidentally hit him in his eye. His eye later turned purple and blue.

"No one ever told me about Hannalore! No one ever told me! It's too much . . . it's too much. . . . I thought she was—" But she was so worn out she couldn't finish her sentence. And as they slowly approached her from a safer distance, Berenice and my father kept saying, "Sarah, Sarah, Sarah," over and over. Finally Berenice caught my mother in her arms and for a moment shook her roughly, then slapped her, as if to say, It was not you who suffered so! It was not you who was dragged into the living darkness, into a living hell! And then Berenice held my mother tight as if she were a baby, for more than anything, Berenice loved my mother. She rocked her gently in her arms.

"Sarah, Sarah. They did terrible things to Hannalore, Sarah. Unspeakable. Worse than what happened to the Cantor. But even so, she was strong and used all her strength to make a new life. She wanted it to be secret while she was alive, and the Cantor promised her. Let her be our Hannalore. Let her be Hannalore."

My mother, exhausted, turned pale. She opened her mouth wide and cursed God.

I came completely out of my isolation the day of Hannalore's unveiling, destroying all remnants and reminders. When we arrived home I cut the coarse red stitches on the curtains and tore the curtains themselves down. I raised the venetian blinds and stood on a chair to unscrew their supports from the top of the frames. One by one they came crashing to the floor. I opened all the windows of my room.

I went outside and offered to help Berenice bring out the palms from the Palmenhaus.

She looked startled when she saw me coming, almost afraid. She had been sitting on her patio, staring into space.

"Oh, God. Thank God," she finally said when I told her why I had come over. "Thank God. Yes, of course. I couldn't do it myself."

"*Y*ou knew about Hannalore," my mother said to me later that day in the living room. I was sweating from the warmth of the sun and the exertion of moving all the palms.

I was silent.

"Berenice told you, didn't she? When? Why? It wasn't good for you to know, not the way you always were or are now. It harmed you. She shouldn't have told you. I can never forgive her for doing that."

At that moment I could not figure out if my mother

actually knew the truth, that Berenice had indeed told me about Hannalore a long time ago.

I was not shocked when I read Hannalore's masculine Hebrew name, since I had known the secret of Hannalore from the time Berenice had taken me on the ride along the Welland Canal, when she had slowed the car and shown me the half picture with the Cantor.

"Hannalore tore herself out of the picture so she would not be reminded of what they did or what she was before. So she could start anew."

After Berenice told me about Hannalore, I put it out of my mind, pretending she had never told me how they operated on a teenage boy and did terrible things to him.

"Berenice told you, didn't she?" my mother repeated.

I was still silent.

I realized my mother could not *know* that Berenice had told me. She could only suspect it, and this made it easier for her to blame someone else for all she feared and for everything that had come to pass since I was a child.

"Silence is an admission," she said. "I will not see Berenice Seidengarn again."

Finally I said, "It did not affect me."

She thought this over for a moment and then spoke calmly, slowly, as if she was only then figuring something out. As if she were talking to a crazy person.

"No, it did not affect you, Alexander. It did not affect you at all. When you turned sixteen you went into your room and have stayed there for a year. Just like a zombie. Walking around the house at night like the living dead—'present tense, eternal tense'—eavesdropping on your father and me! Didn't you ever hear of the subconscious? You did what you did at the same age that the Cantor and Hannalore were first taken away. No. It did not affect you."

"It did not affect me or my subconscious." I, too, spoke calmly, but I was shaken by this bit of information. I had never considered the ages when the Cantor and Hannalore were taken away. I had never imagined them at an age other than those ages when I knew them, when they were no longer young. When I thought of them—and I rarely did—being taken away and about the terrible things done to them, I saw them as they were in my present life, middle-aged people, slightly older than my parents and more worn out than they should have been for their age.

My mother stared at me while I was thinking.

"It did not affect me," I finally repeated.

My mother imitated me. "'It did not affect me. It did not affect me.'" She then lost control. Her voice spiraled up, and she was shouting. "Then how do you explain your behavior at the unveiling! Tell me, Aryeh Alexander! Tell me! How do you explain your crazy outburst at the unveiling! 'C'est vrai, Madame Rabbi!' How?"

She turned and ran out of the room.

And though I understood my mother's pain, and the

fears she allowed to govern her life—for I knew she had real fears to reckon with and fears that appeared to her to have come true—I found it hard to forgive her. I watched helplessly as she broke Berenice's already battered heart.

"Are you angry with me, Sarah?" Berenice would say, coming into my mother's room, where she had taken to her bed as she had all those years before in the summer of her confinement. "What did I do, Sarah? . . . I've always loved you so. I've always loved you so. I'm sorry, I'm sorry." But my mother would not answer her and would turn to the wall. Berenice made several attempts, coming by every day, aided by my father, who would peek his head in their bedroom and announce, "Sarah, Berenice is here. Your dearest friend is here." But Berenice was always rebuffed. "Please, everyone go away. I'm too tired for visitors."

Finally Berenice stopped trying. "Maybe your mother needs time," she told me in our living room, the last day she tried to approach my mother. "It was such a shock for her, Alexander. So many shocks. Maybe all these years I never appreciated what she suffered. I held everyone to a different standard. I was arrogant. . . . How does one dare compare sufferings?" She began crying. "Maybe she'll be herself one day soon . . . maybe she'll be my friend again."

My father came into the room. He spoke slowly, so as not to choke on his words. "She just needs time, Berenice, give her time. . . . I'm sorry. . . . She will be your . . . beloved friend again."

Berenice tried to smile. "Yes, Rabbi, I think you're right. I do."

But Berenice and my father were wrong. They did not really know my mother. For that had always been her way, to withdraw from what frightened her, from the unbearable; to retreat quietly, as she had long ago retreated from me, to hide deep within herself, beyond the intrusive glare of a rational sun, never to return.

Baghdad

*T*he following autumn I went to McGill University, on an island set between two rivers, between the St. Lawrence and the Des Prairies Rivers, which in turn join the Ottawa.

Montreal island was never in my mind shaped like a kiss but rather was like a single flicker of flame. Frozen in time.

I studied not far from the Outremont neighborhood where Berenice had grown up. I was an excellent student. Perhaps my year in confinement made me even more prepared for university life than I would have been had I gone too early and in internal disorder. Though the university at that time was English-speaking, I took courses and learned a proper French, though with an accent like the Quebecois, like Berenice.

After my mother had taken once more to her bed, before I went away for school, she began to believe she was pregnant again. Though she was still young enough to be pregnant, she was not. Dr. Desjarlais said it was a kind of shock. "I've seen this before. I could tell you cases."

My father at first tried to humor her, and as during that summer years before when I went with the Cantor and Berenice to the lake, he treated her as if she were expecting a child. On hot days the windows were left wide open—my mother still did not approve of air-conditioning and thought it might harm the baby. My father placed several fans in the room, and they whirred and whispered, turning their faces to and fro, loyal guardians of the imaginary baby growing in my mother's womb. He filled several vases with flowers from the garden that she had planted—peonies, irises, and roses.

My father was patient and long-suffering, but even he had his limits. After many months, when the summer was long over and the cold autumn weather had set in, he tried gently to talk her out of her delusion.

"Sarah, why are you staying so long in there? It's a mistake. I'm sorry, but we must have lost the baby. Our poor baby. Why don't you come out of our room." He never said that she had simply imagined the baby but always, "I'm sorry, but we must have lost the baby. Our poor baby."

For a long time my mother completely ignored him, and then one day, when he finished saying, "Why don't you come out of our room?" she simply answered, "Well, I guess now it's my turn to be crazy." And she continued to stay in her room.

As the summer months went by, Berenice realized that my mother would never resume their friendship. Berenice told me: "When your mother fixes on an idea, nothing can change her mind. She's the most stubborn person I know."

At the end of summer Berenice put her house up for sale and also sold the necklace that Marla had given Hannalore. Berenice moved abroad to the Galilee. She wanted to be with her brother.

She told me before I left for university: "You know, Alexander, after all this time my brother is the only family I have left, and I hardly know him anymore. I hope he will be good to me. He says he's very happy I'm coming. We got along well when we were children, so I'm hopeful. I know we all change a lot as we get older, but part of us remains the same.

"Well, my brother already has two grandchildren! Can you believe it, Alexander? He's not even fifty!"

She embraced me in her arms and squeezed me as she used to when I was a child.

"I will always consider you and your parents, even your mother, as my real family. I wanted to give you the necklace

Marla gave Hannalore, since Marla was your friend, but I needed the money."

Berenice then held me at arms' length and smiled. "I will always be thankful to that poor girl. Somehow I feel she is looking out for me. What a strange and wonderful guardian angel!

"Will you come see me one day, Alexander? Will you promise? It's far away, but maybe you'll become the traveler your great-grandfather was. You could even write a book."

But it was my father who became a traveler. It was my father who surprised everyone.

At the end of winter, when nine months of my mother's imaginary pregnancy were over, my father asked me to come home for the weekend. As soon as I arrived at the house, he took me into the bedroom he had always shared with my mother. I suppose he needed me for a witness, as he always did after he received some important information from one of his colleagues, when he would move a colored flag pin with the name of some ancient city from one bank of a river to the other.

He said to my mother: "I'm sorry, Sarah. You will have to leave your room. I'm going on a trip. You will have to take care of yourself until I return."

My mother looked wide-eyed at him. She did not look at me. I, too, was stunned.

She said: "Will you come back?"

"Of course. I will only be away for a few months."

That afternoon my mother got dressed and went downstairs for the first time since the day of Hannalore's unveiling. She busied herself in the kitchen, organizing its drawers and cupboards, putting in order her long neglected telephone desk.

My father planned an extensive itinerary that included an initial trip to Iraq and the places along the Euphrates and Tigris Rivers that were the obsession of his adult life. He gave me a list of his expected dates in each place. He would bring his grandfather's book along. Dr. Aschenbach had told him it was very helpful when he went, and my father was very proud of this.

After his visit to Iraq, my father intended to travel to Jerusalem. He told me he planned on going up from there to the Galilee to see Berenice.

"It will be the most important goal of my pilgrimage. Even more important than Jerusalem. Years ago when we all came to Windsor I promised the Cantor that if anything happened to him, I would always look after Berenice. It's time I kept my promise. And if anything should ever happen to me, you must promise to always look after Mother. I know you've not had an easy time with her; her fears confuse her, but despite everything she loves you. She's your mother."

My father's death was as quick as it was unexpected. Two days after he arrived in Baghdad, he took sick. He never left the capital to visit any of the ancient places on his itinerary. We never really understood exactly what happened, but Dr. Desjarlais told us that it sounded like a burst appendix. "If it had happened here he would still be alive!"

After Dr. Desjarlais made numerous calls to the Iraqi Embassy in Ottawa and to various Canadian government agencies, my father's body was allowed to be flown back for burial in Windsor. "It's always a tricky business when you die abroad," Dr. Desjarlais told us.

My mother went around the house placing sheets on the mirrors the way I remembered my father doing the day he told me, "Your mother's brother died, your uncle Avner. You never met him. He was sick for a long time."

My mother did not inform my grandmother in Frankfurt about my father's death. "What difference would it make to that old witch?" my mother said. My mother had begun to speak to me again, gradually but in a distant and distracted way, out of necessity, I suppose.

I called Berenice at her brother's home in the Galilee.

After a long muffled silence, for she must have been crying, Berenice said, "Oh, Alexander, I loved your father so much . . . and your mother will need you now. Be patient with her."

A great multitude gathered at the Sha'arai Rakhamim cemetery for my father's funeral. The people all seemed familiar, though I did not look much around me. In the crowd I thought I saw the parents who had lost their two children on Tecumseh Road, but I was not sure. Perhaps I was imagining it. They seemed frail and worn beyond their possible years. Out of the corner of my eye I spotted some of the older women who would come to call upon my mother during the summer of her confinement, the same women who would get up from their seats, exchange pleasantries, and leave whenever Berenice and I returned from Belle River.

And Mrs. Cook was there.

She emerged from the crowd.

She came over to my mother and me but was so distraught she could not speak. She pressed all our hands together. She suddenly smiled strangely. I looked down and saw that the sapphire on its string had peeked out from between two upper buttons of my shirt, just behind my black tie. The brilliant stone flashed for a moment in the morning sun. Mrs. Cook reached her arm out as if to touch it but then stopped her hand in midair as the gem disappeared back under my shirt. Finally she said, "Marla and I are so glad you have it. It's a righteous stone; I found out its history. It has done good deeds."

When I said the prayers at the graveside, I spoke in the language of earliest times. I said all the words, with their constellations of letters that had once combined themselves this way and that in myriad forms to create all of our souls and to create this world, which is our home.

And while I prayed out loud, the letters hovered before me. They assembled themselves not only into my father, but into the Cantor, Hannalore, Marla, even into Berenice, who was still alive though far away, and into my mother, who took my hand as she wept quietly at my side.

And all six appeared before me in a waking dream, like so many pillars of cloud and pillars of fire, to lead me through my days and to lead me through my nights.

They began to move, one before the other, hand in hand, in a wondrous procession through the crowded Sha'arai Rakhamim. Fire and cloud. Cloud and fire. They beckoned to me, and each other, to that place which remains outside time and this earth, where we might always go to reconcile ourselves.

And what could I believe then but that God's Mercy and Loving-kindness were bound up within all of them. And what choice, what luxury, remained for me, at that moment and on that sanctified ground, but to bless God's Holy Name forevermore.

Acknowledgments

I am grateful to my editor, Celina Spiegel, for her guiding wisdom and generous spirit, and to my wonderful agent, Nina Ryan.

I also wish to thank the following people who in various ways helped and encouraged me during the writing of *The Far Euphrates:* Barbara and Dr. Merton Bernstein, Victor M. DeMattia, Dieter Hall, Mary Jurisson, Shirley Gabis Perle, Henriette Simon Picker, Wendy Ran, and Patricia Sado.

A special debt of gratitude is owed to my dear friend the novelist and memoirist Laura Furman, who has been invaluable in my growth as a writer.